You've Got Aliens

Alienn, Arkansas 1

FIONA ROARKE

YOU'VE GOT ALIENS
ALIENN ARKANSAS 1
Copyright © Fiona Roarke

This book is a work of fiction. The characters, organizations, events, and places portrayed in this book are products of the author's imagination and are either fictitious or are used fictitiously. Any similarity to a real person, living or dead is purely coincidental and not intended by the author.

ISBN: 978-1-944312-12-1

Want to know when Fiona's next book will be available? Sign up for her Newsletter: http://eepurl.com/bONukX

For my family, friends and fans whether near or far, thank you so much for your unwavering and enthusiastic support of my desire to write light, funny Sci-Fi Romance. It's so much fun.

Available Now from Fiona Roarke

BAD BOYS IN BIG TROUBLE
Biker
Bouncer
Bodyguard
Bomb Tech
Bounty Hunter
Bandit

Trouble in Paradise
Barefoot Bay Kindle Worlds

Close Encounters of the Alien Kind
Nocturne Falls Universe 1

ALIENN, ARKANSAS SERIES
You've Got Aliens

Coming Soon:
Invasion of the Alien Snatchers
Nocturne Falls Universe 2

Librarian and aspiring journalist Juliana Masters has a mystery to solve: Who am I? Armed with the truth about her past, she can leave her humdrum present behind and get on with her future. She just needs to complete one lucrative investigative writing assignment and she'll be on her way. All she has to do is prove aliens live and work out of a secret facility based under the Big Bang Truck Stop. No problem. Getting her socks knocked off by the Fearless Leader isn't part of the plan.

Diesel Grey worked for years to achieve his goal of heading up the family business in Alienn, Arkansas. Mission accomplished, but being Fearless Leader of a galactic way station comes with a lot more headaches than anticipated. It's hard to consider the shockingly well-informed writer a headache, though, especially when she makes him ache in all the right places.

If he's not careful, he'll give her everything she needs to blow his family's cover and expose to the human world that aliens do walk among them.

All he really wants to do is sweep her up in his arms and never let her go.

If only his trigger-happy brother would stop erasing her memories.

Chapter 1

The Big Bang Truck Stop, Alienn Arkansas

"No. Absolutely not." Diesel Grey regarded his elderly aunt Dixie Grey with a disbelieving eye. She'd really gone too far this time. As thin as the proverbial rail, his aunt *looked* harmless, but attitude alone made up ninety percent of her body weight. "We have a certain reputation to uphold and—"

Aunt Dixie cut him off. "Stop right there." She fixed a sardonic stare on him as her palm lifted parallel to his chest. "First of all, this is a truck stop not the Vatican. Our standing in the community could use a little upgrade, if you ask me.

"Second of all, I wear a silver lamé skirt every day of my life with my hind end hanging out for all the world to see at the Cosmos Café. Do not preach to me about our reputation." She lifted the other hand to put air quotes around the word "reputation" as if she didn't believe they had a good one. He noticed her long, decoratively lacquered, over-the-top nails. They were hard to miss.

The Nebula Nail Salon, located on Main Street in downtown Alienn Arkansas, was known for its far-out, celestial designs. Currently Aunt Dixie had a swirly, sparkly lavender, white and green base design mimicking a galaxy with tiny 3-D planets affixed to the end of each nail, making it seem like ten little planets revolved around her fingertips. For a moment, he couldn't take his eyes off them, but needed to respond.

He took a deep breath. "First of all, what you're proposing doesn't even come close to qualifying as an upgrade to our current standing in the community. And second of all, *you* were the one who cut eight inches off your skirt, making it shorter than the uniform of any other waitress in the cafe to show off your assets, as you so expressively call them, much to my dismay. Do not act like I made you do it."

Eyes flashing, Aunt Dixie said, "Hey, the shorter the skirt, the bigger the tips. Everybody knows that."

"Fine, whatever. But your hind end hangs out every day because of your choices, not mine. You can't throw that on me."

"Sure I can."

"How do you figure that?" He resisted the urge to cross his arms over his chest, guessing it would make him look too preachy. He also purposely stretched his fingers to keep from making fists. Balling up his hands would definitely make him look hostile, a look he knew wouldn't help this situation in the least.

Diesel watched as his aunt searched the ceiling for a moment as if it would give her the perfect sarcastic retort to make her point. Her head dropped briefly, then slowly lifted as her expression hardened. "I am your elder, Diesel. Elders are to be respected. That means my word is law."

He lost the battle of not looking hostile. Rolling his eyes, he dropped his gaze to stare at his aunt. "I do respect you as my elder, Aunt Dixie. However, a wet T-shirt contest at the old folks' home to promote the Big Bang Truck Stop is a bad idea on so many levels I can't name the top ten contenders in a logical order. And hear me when I tell you that I won't allow it."

She drew a big breath to continue the argument, but he leaned forward across his desk.

"Contrary to your views on elders, *I* am the one in charge here, so *my* word is actually law. Therefore, you may not use our truck stop logo T-shirts in this manner. Nor will I donate them for any project of this nature. Think of something else for your new fundraiser. I know—how about a nice bake sale?"

"Killjoy!" Aunt Dixie turned and stomped off toward three other elderly women waiting just inside the open door to his office.

"Sorry, girls, the wet T-shirt contest is a no-go, thanks to Mr. Spoilsport over there." A ringed-planet thumbnail shot over her shoulder to gesture in his direction. "We'll have to think up another fundraiser for the old folks' home, and it will *not* be a stupid bake sale."

"Boo! Hiss!" the other ladies all hurled in his direction. Mrs. Green even stuck her tongue out. He didn't take it to heart. He knew they wouldn't hold a grudge…well, they wouldn't hold it for very long. He hoped.

Diesel had never expected to be popular as the one in charge and he'd been right. In the here and now with a foursome of elderly ladies booing and hissing him, he could only do his best not to laugh. He pasted on a tolerant smile as they filed out of his office. There were days when his most difficult chore was not rolling his eyes every five seconds at a task or problem facing him.

As soon as his "elders" exited, his brother entered with a piece of thick, gray message paper in his hand. "Guess what?" Axel asked, staring down at the page he carried.

"No."

Axel looked up sharply. "No? Why? What's your problem?"

"You just passed them on the way in."

His brother laughed. "So you officially turned down the wet T-shirt contest at the old folks' home, huh?"

Diesel shouldn't be surprised, but asked, "How did you know about that?"

Axel shrugged. "They asked me first. I told them they had to ask you."

"Why?"

"They knew for a fact you'd turn them down. I'm a softer touch. They always come to me first. Didn't you know that?" Axel's brows curved inward as if he were puzzled by Diesel's complete lack of understanding as to the way things worked.

"Yes, I knew that. But why would you do that to me, Bro? Next time, it's your turn to nix their outlandish idea of the day."

"No, thanks. That's why you get the big bucks."

"Wait a minute. Does that mean you knew about last month's fundraiser scheme for the pin-up silver fox candid calendar?"

Axel laughed until tears actually filled his eyes. "Now that would have been a humdinger of a moneymaker, wouldn't it?"

"Some kind of dinger, anyway." That observation only made Axel laugh harder. One day, Diesel thought, he was going to roll his eyes back so hard, they'd stick and stay lodged upward forever.

Axel finally wiped his eyes and handed over the paper he'd brought up from the communications center downstairs. The gray color meant it was a high priority message. Diesel hoped it wasn't bad news from their home planet, Alpha-Prime. His brother *was* uncharacteristically joyful, so maybe he could relax on that front.

"Check it out. We got it!"

"What did we get?" Diesel studied the paper, gaze fixing immediately on the initials UGG—United Galactic Gulag—centered at the top of the page.

"The detention route contract." Axel sounded very proud of himself.

Diesel huffed. This was dubious good news at best. He set the sheet of paper down on top of the dozens of others on the desk in front of him. "You mean the Galactic Gulag Run?" he asked sardonically.

Axel sighed. "I hear the disdain in your tone. Don't be difficult. This is good for us. The money this deal brings in will help keep us operational and more viable as a way station in this area of the galaxy."

"We're already operational. What's wrong with simply being a galactic way station for space travelers on their way to nice vacation destinations instead of the big house?"

"We're too far out from the popular vacation routes nowadays. This quadrant of space isn't hip anymore."

"Not hip?" Diesel started to roll his eyes, but stopped and shook his head. He needed to find a better way to vent his annoyance. If he didn't, he'd go blind or spend the rest of his life staring at his brain.

He took a deep breath and attempted a more positive approach. Perhaps yoga was the answer to combating his growing stress.

"The Paradise Planet is a beautiful tropical place to vacation—"

"Yes. And it was *awesome* for our grandparents. But now we're competing with adventurous vacation destinations for the younger generation like the Gothic Ice Floe Planet and Lava Rock World, both of which are in the Tri-Spiral Galaxy way on the other side of this galaxy. We've had this discussion before. I thought you were on board."

"I am. You're right. This is good for us." His tone sounded impossibly forlorn to his own ears.

"So why the resistance?"

Diesel looked up at his brother. He wasn't getting information he hadn't heard before. He knew he was merely parroting the voices of the current council of elders.

He was in charge. He did have the final word, but the council—made up of retired former leaders of the Big Bang Truck Stop and its alien underground operation—always wanted their voices and opinions considered.

Every single one of the elders' minds was firmly planted in the past, as were their strict ideas for this venture. At one time or another, each of the elders had been in a position of power—either upstairs or down—before retiring to a position on the council.

His father was a council member, but spent

much of his time traveling the country with Diesel's mother, Xenia. Zebulon Grey understood Diesel's leadership issues since he'd once faced his fair share, and generally left his eldest son to it. Diesel hoped he'd be just as reasonable when the younger generation took over. Perhaps he'd also travel far, wide and continually like his parents in their spiffy new RV.

Diesel and Axel, along with their brothers Cam, Wheeler, Gage and Jack and even little sister Valene, all knew the future in this part of the Milky Way was ever-changing. They needed to adapt and change with it or become obsolete. Alpha-Prime, in the Caldera Forte Galaxy, wouldn't let them simply operate as the Big Bang Truck Stop, the largest full-service refueling station in south central Arkansas. There had to be something worthwhile for them beyond the single reason their people had come here so long ago. While profits from their business made the Greys successful by Earth standards, and in the surrounding area of Arkansas, the ruling party on their planet always wanted improvement.

"The Bauxite mine will always keep our people in the area," Axel said out loud. "Folks on Alpha-Prime will always need fuel." Diesel would volunteer to stay, as would his brothers and every other off-world-born resident of Alienn, Arkansas.

"But we both know it would only take a handful of the folks from our planet to handle the mine alone," Diesel said. "We also need to keep the way station viable for galactic citizens traveling in this region of space. Any regularly scheduled traffic only helps our goal to stay on this planet."

"Because we like Earth and we want to live here forever, right?"

"Yes. We do."

Earth was a great assignment. The more Alphas who lived here, the more people from Alpha-Prime they needed to keep things running. If more people visited or volunteered to live and work here, they might realize the perks, but so far only a small portion of their out-of-this-world visitors had ever ventured beyond the truck stop into the beautiful landscape of Arkansas, much less the country. The last person to voluntarily come to Earth to work and live was their orphaned cousin, Stella Grey.

Typical visitors to Alienn's way station were all understandably impatient to get on to their galactic vacation destinations. The few who wanted to explore Earth had to go through a rather elaborate procedure to procure a guide and understand the rules they all lived by here on Earth, the primary one being that no human could know aliens lived among them and had for years.

Only a handful of extraterrestrial visitors had gone through the necessary and lengthy procedures to get a permit to explore beyond the safety zone that was the truck stop.

Alpha-Prime's strict colonization prerogative kept their people's numbers on Earth restricted so as not to reveal their existence and promptly rile up the indigenous population, or rather, the *puny earthlings*, as the ruling party members always said under their breath during discussions of Earth. They were only partly kidding about the nickname.

Humans tended to have quite a strong reaction to exposure to extraterrestrials and not always in a positive way.

The colonization prerogative of Alpha-Prime was mostly in place for planets where Alphas permanently resided and the indigenous population was aware of their existence.

Earth had not been so categorized. The Alpha community on Earth had started as a mining colony, but they'd maintained the truck stop for nearly as long. Earth was not even on the list for the indigenous population to be notified as to their presence in the near or even distant future. As far as the home planet and the elders who'd retired on Earth were concerned, it would remain that way for quite some time. The ruling party members on Alpha-Prime were not convinced earthlings were ready to accept aliens in their midst.

Diesel mostly agreed with that assessment, but once in a while he wished their existence was out in the open. He had several human friends and wished he didn't feel like he was lying to them by omission each time they conversed.

Meanwhile, the elder council was here to ensure he and any future Fearless Leader kept with the old ways of secrecy as much as possible. That meant the council members poked their retired noses into his business every chance they got and any manner of change was usually met with indignation at best, outrage the rest of the time.

Diesel said, "I wish the elder council was more agreeable to any kind of variation in our routine. We so much as change the scheduled gelatin flavor at the Cosmos Café on any given day and there is a mass organized protest—usually with Aunt Dixie, protest sign in hand, leading the way ready to sanction me for crimes against humanity."

Axel grunted. "Wish in one hand and poop in the other and see which fills up first."

"Stop with the hillbilly proverbs."

Axel shrugged. "Stop wishing for foolish things."

"Change is not foolish. Until I took over last year, nothing much had changed since our people arrived on Earth."

"So?"

"So things are different. Thanks to advances in human technology, now we have to do a better job of hiding our existence from the population, but the councils here and on Alpha-Prime don't seem to get it.

"If we get found out and anyone can prove it or we don't erase their memories quickly enough, the rulers on Alpha-Prime will yank our operation out of here so fast our heads will spin off, then use an experimental Defender bomb to level the place and ensure local memories of our very existence are forever erased."

"So break it to the council gently," Axel said. "You're good at handling them, Diesel. That's why we voted you into the job."

"I'm the eldest in our family and I worked my butt off to be in charge. That's why I'm here, not because of any vote."

"That you know of." Axel grinned and Diesel relaxed. His brother was just winding him up. He took another deep breath and read the few words on the contract signature page for the Galactic Gulag Run.

"If you explain the reasons why this is so important, the council will understand." Axel tilted his head and added, "Or they'll boo and hiss and stick their tongues out at you, but you've already survived that kind of torture more than once."

That was the truth. Anytime Aunt Dixie and her friends were involved in an unpopular decision, they always booed, they always hissed and someone *always* stuck their tongue out at him.

"Right." Diesel studied the gray paper again, rereading it quickly.

"What are you going to do?" Axel asked.

"I'll sign the contract and tell them all about it later. Better to beg for forgiveness than ask for permission, right?"

Axel looked dubious. "Sure, Bro, whatever you think."

Diesel thought he'd rather consign himself to the worst prison in the United Galactic Gulag system and spend the rest of his life doing hard labor, sledgehammering granite-like boulders down to pea gravel, than break this news to the council of elders.

Axel was right, though. This was a good contract for their purposes. It would add significantly to the bottom line of his Earth-bound colony.

Often he secretly asked himself, *What would my father do?*

He well knew his father had once tried to procure the same type of prison contract, but had been shot down by the council. His father had stopped asking them anything important soon after and advised Diesel to do the same.

Zeb Grey had been one of the best leaders the colony had ever had. Diesel had big space boots to fill when his parent retired, but he knew his father had been very ready to step down and let him take over. His mother wanted to travel across the country. His father, as always, wanted to indulge her. Currently his parents were somewhere in the continental U.S. in an RV enjoying their retirement.

Diesel knew his father might have signed the UGG contract without any input from anyone else, if retirement hadn't been on his horizon. He'd left the decision to Diesel, because he was the one who'd have to deal with it in the long run.

Diesel signed the document with a flourish, agreeing to the ten-year contract for a monthly service run from Alpha-Prime in the Caldera Forte Galaxy to the prison planet XkR-9, in the Andromeda Galaxy by way of the Milky Way and Earth. It would be steady, regular income for the next ten years, making it harder for Alpha-Prime to shut them down on a whim. Plus, the way station would receive a generous stipend for each and every UGG ship beyond the scheduled monthly run that landed here for service, rest and relaxation during the long trip between galaxies.

Before Axel left the room, Diesel's assistant, Nova Greene, raced into his office. She looked distressed. *Now what?* He should've called in sick, even though their kind never got sick in the way humans did.

"What is it, Nova?" he asked, mentally bracing for yet another chaotic issue this evening.

"There's a young woman out here asking for you."

"Who is it?"

Nova's already large eyes widened and rounded as she whispered, "It's a human."

Diesel put a finger on the pinch of pain above his right eye. Not hiding his annoyance, he asked, "Could you be a little bit more specific, Nova? There are quite a few humans roaming around on this planet." He saw Axel bite down on the inside of his cheek but fail to stop the large smile that shaped his mouth. Diesel gave him a stern look and he subdued his amusement.

Nova pushed out a long sigh. "She says her name is Juliana Masters."

"And you don't believe her?"

"Oh, I believe her all right. I also know she's about to be very big trouble."

"How do you know that?"

"I read her mind."

Axel, unable to hold in his inappropriate amusement any longer, laughed until he had to wipe away the tears rolling out of his eyes again. "I love coming to your office," he said. "It never fails to entertain."

Diesel inhaled deeply and exhaled slowly. "I told you to stop doing that, Nova. It unnerves folks, most especially human folk."

"Be that as it may, she has lots of questions swirling around in that pretty head of hers." Nova tapped the side of her temple with a finger indicating where the human's questions were *swirling* around.

"Questions about the truck stop?" Diesel wasn't opposed to answering questions about their "human" business. It was very successful for an Earth-bound venture and he was proud they'd sustained it for so long as a profitable business enterprise. It was also the only subject he could talk about in all honesty with humans.

"No. She's got a boatload of questions about—"

Nova lowered her voice as if the whole world might hear, "—*the rumors*."

"The rumors? What specific rumors are we talking about?" He mentally pushed out a very long sigh. He already had a good idea what rumors, but there were a few choices and he needed to hear her say it.

Protocol was protocol.

Every place had rumors. He didn't believe anyone truly knew anything of importance, though. Then again, given his day so far, perhaps he should knock on wood to ward off any evil luck about to come his way. Too bad he wasn't in the least superstitious.

"You know, Diesel. The rampant rumors of space beings living and working around the Big Bang Truck Stop and in the nearby town of Alienn, Arkansas, along with the vast conspiracy theories of why cellular service doesn't work for ten miles in any direction here."

Chapter 2

Juliana Masters sat in the cramped reception area of the Big Bang Truck Stop manager's office, waiting for an audience with the man in charge of this place. There were only two chairs, and one was the receptionist's. Juliana was apparently next in line after an attractive man carrying a gray piece of paper like it was a sacred scroll went in without consulting the receptionist. Four elderly women had exited, seemingly in a bad temper, and Mr. Gray Paper had nodded politely at each of the fearsome foursome as they passed.

Nova, the receptionist, had stared at Juliana intently for quite a long time before scurrying off to ask her boss if he was available for an interview.

One of the seniors, a feisty-looking lady with very ornate fingernails that featured what looked like 3-D planets on each tip, glanced at Juliana.

Leaning down, she said, "Whatever you're here to ask, don't get your hopes up. He's in an especially foul mood today." She turned to her friends. "Come on, girls. Let's get back to town and try to think up another idea for a fundraiser."

If the manager was already in a foul mood, maybe this impromptu visit had been a bad idea. Then again, she needed the manager's cooperation. She was certain he had information she couldn't get anywhere else to confirm or reasonably debunk all the rumors she'd heard about the large truck stop and the town of Alienn. She needed a reliable source to help her find the truth.

For starters, how did Alienn, Arkansas get its name? Could it truly be so obvious? Were there aliens living here? It seemed like a bad way to hide, but perhaps it was brilliant in its simplicity. If there were aliens roaming around, how long had they been here? If not, was the whole alien theme only a marketing gimmick?

One way or another, she planned to find out so she could finish her article and send it in to Finder's. She could really use the big payoff the popular travel magazine and blog had promised if she completed the special assignment and either proved the existence of aliens, past or present, in Alienn, or found some other interesting reason why Alienn, Arkansas should be included in her article.

Finder's wanted to do a book on extra-special places to visit, where unique possibilities of alien or strange happenings had been proven or at least not completely debunked. There had been rumors for years that extraterrestrials were running around Alienn, Arkansas, but Juliana didn't believe them.

Her take was that secrets were very difficult to keep. If there were truly aliens in residence here, someone would have outed them a long time ago and made a ton of money or debunked the rumors and, well…probably made a ton of money. It was the general lack of substantial proof either way that she found the most intriguing.

Juliana reached into her pocket, pulled out her cell phone and checked to ensure that indeed she had zero service here. That was one thing she'd love to figure out once and for all. Why was there no service for a ten-mile radius around the town of Alienn, which included the truck stop on its southern edge by Route 88? It could be her closing argument. She'd be done and then she could finish this article, get paid and get on with her life. Such as it was.

Her phone had gone from full bars to no bars the moment she'd gotten within exactly ten miles of the truck stop. That's also where the signs started. The blatantly large, very well-lit billboards could not be missed as travelers made their way toward Alienn, Arkansas and the Big Bang Truck Stop.

Maxwell the Martian, a short, scrawny-bodied cartoon alien with gray skin, a big head, lively oversized blue eyes and a smile shaping his small mouth, started extolling the virtues of the Big Bang Truck Stop, only ten miles ahead, with the very first sign.

Every mile all the way toward the town limits of Alienn, Arkansas, was a different billboard with Maxwell the Martian proclaiming the amazing accolades of the truck stop. For example, "Stop in Alienn for out of this world prices!"; "Keep on Truckin' to Alienn, Arkansas for gas and snacks so you can keep on truckin' to your favorite destination!"; and "Alienn, Arkansas…Where you get a Big Bang for your Buck!"

She'd been intrigued and amused, reading each sign out loud as she drove along the highway, forgetting momentarily about her lack of phone service. Soon it would be dusk, and depending on how long this took, she'd definitely be driving home in the dark. At least it was less than an hour back home to Doraydo.

In the distance, maybe half a mile from the Big Bang Truck Stop, the town's water tower was eye-catching in the fading sunlight. The tank was cleverly painted to look like a flying saucer with a 3-D version of Maxwell the Martian hanging off the side as if for dear life, but with his signature goofy smile in place as if he merely rode an amusement park roller coaster and not an out-of-control space craft about to crash to Earth.

This whole place was over the top. The truck stop itself was probably half the size of the small town of Alienn, perched on the edge of the city limits on the semi-major Route 88 that connected Mississippi and Texas through southern Arkansas.

Juliana had inquired about the manager at the convenience store. It was seemingly the hub of the whole place, given that it was a truck stop and the primary reason people stopped in town was for fuel.

The name Diesel Grey had been whispered behind a hand when she met with Pete Harriman, who'd assigned her to write the tell-all article. Mr. Harriman would proffer her piece to Finder's for evaluation and inclusion in the next special edition travel book. He was one of the editors for the project.

Mr. Harriman, one of her former teachers at the university in Doraydo, whispered most of the information as if the space aliens he believed in might be listening in on their conversation some way, somehow.

She was dubious about each and every word he said, but she figured that would make her article all the more credible. "Once I was a disbeliever, but now I see the truth. Aliens do walk among us and here's my proof." Or something like that.

Unless she didn't find anything credible. Then her article would be more factual, the *discover for yourself if all the rumors are truly debunked* approach.

Either way, she simply wanted to get the promised large paycheck and…well, get on with her life. Maybe she needed to adopt the truck stop's slogan as a personal motto for life: keep on truckin'.

From hidden speakers in every part of the truck

stop she'd visited so far, '80s music, and only '80s music, played non-stop. Juliana found herself bobbing her head to a raucous oldies tune belted out by Cyndi Lauper. She had to forcefully make her body stop wanting to bop to the music.

The convenience store clerk who had directed Juliana to the manager's office wore a nametag that said: Welcome, Earthling! My name is Paulo. He'd pointed toward a good-sized hallway at the back corner of the building. Past the Space Gals and Space Guys bathrooms, an arched doorway opened into a room to the right. The hallway continued through a second archway to, Juliana assumed, the manager's office, judging by the humorous sign mounted above the door. Apparently in keeping with the truck stop's extraterrestrial theme, he wasn't the manager, but the Fearless Leader. Perfect.

She wondered what kind of man Diesel Grey was. When she'd asked the receptionist—her Welcome, Earthling nametag helpfully identified her as Nova—at the pin-neat desk if she could speak to the manager, the woman paused for quite a long time before finally asking, "You mean you'd like to speak to Our Fearless Leader?"

Juliana nodded politely.

Nova was a bit strange and off-putting for a receptionist. She stared at Juliana so intently she wondered sardonically if she'd been mind-probed. Or was the receptionist trying to scare her off with an angry look? Good luck with that. Juliana needed Diesel Grey's cooperation to complete this article. She hoped he'd be willing to send her into a new direction that would help ensure her write-up could be included in the book. She wanted to find one little piece of unproven information to include in her article. Or perhaps a tiny, tantalizing fact that readers wouldn't be able to prove or disprove for themselves. And it would be great if it was info no one else had ever discovered.

That would be perfect. It was unlikely, but she could dream.

A single heated look from a receptionist wasn't going to scare her off. Not much was going to scare her off unless a strange creature with slimy gray skin and three eyes walked up and introduced itself. But she didn't actually believe in aliens from outer space, so she felt fairly safe in the thesis of her article so far. Her take: it was likely all a big suggestive hoax to make a buck.

She'd gotten all of her background information from a source Mr. Harriman had spoken to. His name was Norm—no last name given—and Juliana had sworn never to reveal that this source had talked. As if she could.

Juliana didn't know who the person was, had no way to find out and she wasn't certain if the most scandalous tidbit would stand up to scrutiny. All she had were a few notes that Mr. Harriman had scribbled down on the back of a bar napkin based on his conversation with Norm. It was so outlandish it couldn't possibly be true, but she was ready to give it a shot.

It might be the one thing she could use to put her article over the edge and into the publish pile for the book deal.

"Wait here," Nova had said after a few more seconds of close scrutiny. She hurried through the second archway toward the office of the man...or whatever was in charge of this place.

Waiting for the Fearless Leader of the Big Bang Truck Stop had given her idle time to check her phone repeatedly. She truly did not have a single thread of service. Not a blip. Not even a whisper. Her phone wasn't even trying to find a signal anymore. *Stupid useless thing.* She tucked it back in her purse out of sight and took out her steno pad and pen.

If nothing else, she could at least find out the reason for the lack of cellular service in the area. Did the whole township and the truck stop really only have hard-wired lines? In this day and age?

She didn't know what she'd been expecting the Fearless Leader to look like. Maybe a life-sized version of Maxwell the Martian in a bad Halloween costume, or a guy with skin painted the color of old gravestones. The tall, handsome man who strolled out to greet her was completely unexpected. She stood up on surprisingly weak legs as he approached.

He had dark blond hair, vivid blue eyes, a five o'clock shadow covering his solid jaw and chin, plus a wide, engaging smile that almost made her forget her own name. Unlike every other employee she'd seen, he wasn't wearing silver lamé, but a blue denim shirt open at the throat, nicely fitted black jeans and hiking boots.

There was no sign of Nova. Not that Juliana would have spared the other woman a glance right now.

"Hello. I'm Diesel Grey. I'm in charge of the Big Bang Truck Stop. What can I do for you today…Juliana, is it?" He extended his hand and grasped her fingers in a firm grip. She literally felt a bit of spark when their hands connected. And she liked it, holding on way too long. She also stared at his face for way too long.

He seemed to recognize the flash of the connection. His gaze darted to their hands before leaping back to her eyes.

She finally released his hand and looked down at her steno pad as if holding her own version of an alien artifact, trying to remember why she was here. Juliana took a deep breath and pulled the pen from the spiral wire of the well-used notebook to stall for time. Her embarrassingly girly notions of attraction refused to fade.

Unsure of the level of professionalism she'd exhibit at the moment, she pressed forward anyway.

"Yes. That's right. Juliana Masters." She cleared

her throat and chanced a look into his face again. "I'm a writer working on an article for Finder's for a special book project," she managed to say without her voice hitting a high tenor, squeaking or going out altogether. It was a miracle.

His eyes narrowed slightly, as if he couldn't possibly figure out why she was here to see him, but his engaging smile remained undiminished. She hoped he wouldn't kick her out when she told him what she wanted.

"And how can I help you with that?"

"I'd like to ask you about the rumors surrounding Alienn, Arkansas."

"Rumors?" His voice had a deep timbre. It was sexy, very easy to listen to and…what had she asked?

His smile widened to a grin, the expression giving his already handsome features a whole new beautiful visage. Words dried up in her throat. Her head was no help—nothing at all in there—as she stared at him for way, way too long again.

"What rumors are you talking about?" he clarified. His tone was amused, as if he knew exactly what she was going to ask and was planning on making her say the words out loud.

Touché.

She cleared her throat again but lowered her gaze and said, "The rumors that, one, aliens already live among us and they have for quite some time without being discovered and that, two, you and your entire extended family living in Alienn are from another planet." Her gaze lifted to his face as she completed her volatile sentence.

His smile faded to zero humor. His brows furrowed sternly. Even his frown was attractive. "Sorry, puny earthling. I can't allow you to reveal our secret plan to infiltrate and take over this planet." He put two fingers to his temple. "Now I'll have to use my mind control ability to make you forget why you're here and send you on your way none the wiser."

Juliana sucked in an audible breath. He stared into her eyes, unblinking and serious for three solid seconds.

Did he really think he could control her mind? She closed her eyes, bracing to fight off an alien mind probe, ready to concentrate on keeping her thoughts alive and all hers. When nothing out of the ordinary happened, she squeezed her eyelids tighter and waited some more.

After a few more seconds, he whispered, "Is it working? Do you remember your name or why you've come here, puny earthling?"

Juliana's eyes popped open to see his reacquired and very amused expression. She resisted the urge to sigh out loud as she realized she was being made fun of.

She understood why. It was foolish to have started out the way she did. "Very funny."

"I don't mean to hurt your feelings, but I couldn't seem to resist." He lowered his fingers from his temple and crossed his arms. Somehow this made him look even taller and more masculine and more handsome.

Shake it off, girl. He's only a man.

As she thought it, another half-smile formed on his lips and his eyes seemed to liven with interest. *Stop it. He can't read your mind.*

She shook off her paranoia. "No. That's okay. I had that coming."

"Are you really writing an article for a special Finder's book project?"

"Yes. Of course. It's in conjunction with the university I just graduated from. That's how I got the job."

"Can you prove it?"

"Prove I'm with the university or Finder's?"

"Either one."

Juliana let out a single bark of laughter, but reached for her purse when his inquisitive expression didn't change. She'd just accused him of being an alien from another planet with an alarming agenda. The least she could do was prove she was legit and not some irrational, persecuted crazy person on a journey of insanity.

Pushing aside her useless cell phone, she grabbed her wallet and pulled out the ID part. On one side was a business card from Finder's. On the other, behind the clear plastic holder, was her recent student ID. She held that out for his perusal.

He leaned forward and studied it for quite a long time. There wasn't much on there, just a bad picture that looked like she'd arrived at the registration desk after a drunken lost weekend for a photo that would haunt her for her entire college career. It also featured her date of birth, major field of study, the official school logo, and a student number next to a bar code that gave her access to campus facilities. It wasn't technically valid, since it was fall and she'd graduated at the end of the spring semester. Either way, Diesel seemed to be memorizing it. Was he about to say something disparaging about her awful picture? She yanked her hand back, breaking his concentration.

"Did you get all that?" she asked, wondering what he'd been so focused on.

"I think so. Thanks. Interesting picture. It almost looks like you."

"Be that as it may, you can see I *was* a student. I do have a diploma, but I don't have it with me. Finally, I also have a Finder's editorial number if you want to call and check up on me."

"That won't be necessary and I did see that you were a student."

"Yes. My major was in communications."

"I saw that listed as well. Did you study alien communications, by chance?" His brow quirked up, as did one corner of his mouth. Was there nothing about him she didn't find attractive? Juliana was off her game.

"Not yet. Maybe next time I go to college." In fact, she was done with higher education for now. She planned to finish this article, deposit a big fat check in her account, and set out on a long-awaited trip back to the Northwest. And eventually she wanted a family and a life that wasn't so solitary.

"What do you want, specifically? Are you expecting me to outline my alien plan to take over Earth? I'm not sure I can, because that's very highly classified."

"You're so funny." She forced herself to relax, put a smile on her face and try not to take offense at his continued teasing.

"Thanks. It helps to have a sense of humor in this job. What is it you think I can help you with, Juliana?"

I love the way you say my name.

His smile widened and the force of his stare increased. He was seriously hot.

"Mostly, I wondered if there were any big incidents in the area's past that could have caused rumors like those swirling around Roswell. From what I hear, you're really plugged into everything that goes on around here. That's why I thought you could help me. Was there something odd or unexplained that gave Alienn, Arkansas its reputation for being a haven for extraterrestrials?

Any UFO crashes? Or mass abductions reported locally? Anything like that? I've looked at some historical records, of course, but nothing jumps out. Perhaps I'm not looking in the right place, or nothing was written down and all the good stories are oral ones. If I could have some little-known fact to include in my article, it would really help me out."

Diesel Grey—*what a name*—shrugged. "Well, I personally believe it's the name our small town was given that gets people talking. Technically, we were named after the woman who founded the place over a hundred years ago. Her name was Alienne Greenly." He spelled it out, but pronounced it *I-lean,* with a slight Arkansas-flavored Southern twang. She liked *that* quite a lot, too. "When the official papers were drawn up, somebody wrote down Alienn instead, dropping that last E." He shrugged again, lifting one muscular shoulder and letting it drop.

"Quite a mistake *somebody* made all those years ago."

"True. No one ever said why the E was left off the end, although I suspect laziness on some bygone bureaucrat's part. Maybe by the time they realized the small mistake, the papers had been officially filed and it was too late to change it. Or there was a cost associated and they didn't want to spend the money." He flashed another killer grin and she swore her knees weakened. "But I will say that for whatever reason, it has been awesome for our marketing department for many years now."

"I'll bet it is." Juliana returned his grin with a sincere one of her own. "Maxwell the Martian is obviously quite well known all along Route 88 in southern Arkansas."

He nodded and cocked his head to one side. "Want to meet him?"

"Maxwell the Martian?"

"Yes."

She tilted her head to one side as well. "Is it you and you're about to shapeshift into a scrawny three-foot-tall alien with big blue eyes? Because I *would* really love to see that. Also, will you allow me to record it on my phone?" She started to dig around in her purse one-handed.

He shook his head ruefully. "Sorry, I'd never show you any shapeshifting skills on a first date."

Juliana stared into his expressive, beautiful face. "Is that what this is? A first date?"

"I find it interesting that the part you latched onto was the possible first date and not any shapeshifting skills I may have."

"You've already tried to destroy my memories with your alien mind control. If you could shapeshift, you probably would have done so already to scare me off."

"Well, I guess you've got me there." Another toe-curling smile shaped his lips. "Maxwell is down there." He pointed over her shoulder at the end of the hallway to an end cap display she hadn't noticed on her way in.

She *did* notice he hadn't confirmed or denied whether this interlude was a first date. Perhaps this was dating alien-style. *I should be so lucky.*

They walked down the hallway side by side. Her arm bumped into his a couple of times as they moved, sending a thrill down her spine each time they connected. *Whew.* She needed to calm down.

A small, telephone booth-shaped box with a square glass top stood flush against the end cap. She realized it was similar to an old-fashioned fortune-teller booth. Put a dime in the slot and the fortune teller would shoot out a card from below so you could get a glimpse into your future.

In this case, instead of a turbaned soothsayer behind the glass, a three-foot-high Maxwell the Martian doll occupied the space, complete with a goofy big-eyed stare, infectious grin and one finger pointing at a button on the face of the box.

"What do I have to do, put in some money?"

"Nope, just push the big red button with the palm of your hand." Diesel took her wrist and placed her palm against the four-inch-wide button. His fingers slid over the back of her hand to exert enough force to push the button.

The connection between the two of them was electric. If her hand wasn't covered by his, it would be visibly shaking.

He moved close, hovering over her, their bodies

almost but not quite touching. At least, not at first. Maxwell started moving in a jerky fashion and Diesel leaned in behind her, exerting more pressure on her hand.

When he made first contact with his chest against her shoulder, she inhaled deeply, taking in a big dose of his wonderful scent. His chest remained connected to her back, his palm pressed firmly on her hand. He was warm and tall and he smelled really good. Inside the box, Maxwell's lips started moving in a jerky, mechanical fashion.

"Bing Boing Boppity Bop Boing Bing Bing!" Maxwell said.

Diesel kept his hand on hers for five more seconds until a small gray slip of paper the size of a business card shot out of a slot next to the button.

"There you go." He slowly pulled his hand from hers, easing his chest away from her back. She immediately missed his touch.

Juliana reached for the card, unwilling to admit her hand trembled slightly from the recent contact with the Fearless Leader.

On one side of the gray business card was the Big Bang Truck Stop logo, a semi-truck with the words *keep on truckin'* on the side panel coming around a ringed planet. Along the bottom, a message said, "Welcome, Earthling! Present this card to the cashier for a 5% discount on gas!"

"Awesome, a coupon." Her tone did not convey a single shred of enthusiasm.

"Look on the other side. That's where your official Maxwell the Martian fortune will be."

She flipped the card over, expecting to see something like, "You will meet a tall, gorgeous stranger." *Already have, thank you very much.*

A short rumble of laughter sounded from Diesel's chest, but he only smiled when she glanced over her shoulder at him. Juliana focused on the words printed on the card and felt her cheeks heat: "Maxwell the Martian says, Our Fearless Leader thinks you're very pretty, too."

Chapter 3

Diesel shouldn't have put his hand on Juliana's for the fortune. He really shouldn't have continually read her mind as they stood together. And he was truly walking on the edge of catastrophe by projecting his feelings into the fortune she got.

He studied her again, like he'd been doing pretty much since meeting her in front of Nova's desk. He mentally walked down the list of all the things he liked about her so far. Her hair was a beautiful blonde color.

A strand had brushed his cheek when he'd helped her with the fortune, proving it was as silky and soft as it looked. She was taller than the average human female. Perhaps six or seven inches shorter than his six foot four height.

Her body was slender, but not too skinny. She was absolutely curvy in all the right places. Her smile was captivating and flashed instantly when she was amused. Plus, she wasn't afraid to laugh at herself. He liked talking to her, even though he'd have to watch what he said.

She turned toward him, a really adorable blush staining her cheeks. "You think I'm pretty?" *No. I think you're exquisite.*

He forced a strong shake of his head to keep from admitting the truth out loud. Pointing to the glass box, he said, "Maxwell does."

"But aren't you the Fearless Leader?"

Yes. "Sometimes. Not always."

"Maybe I need to speak to someone else then."

He almost shouted the denial, but managed to speak in a civil tone. "No. You can talk to me." He focused, trying to clearly read her specific intent and ensure it wasn't nefarious. He held his breath as he waited to confirm the vague impression he'd registered earlier when he took a quick look into her very pretty head to ensure she wasn't a true threat.

For some reason he couldn't get a good read on her particular motives. He typically got strong initial impressions when he peeked inside human minds and could usually figure out anyone's primary intent.

Juliana was different. She was harder to read in some ways, easier in others. He clearly understood she thought he was attractive, but the part about her general motives for asking questions at the truck stop was cloudy. Could be for her Finder's article, as she said. If not, what was her primary motive?

Looking into the human mind to assess threats

was often an imprecise practice, especially for his limited abilities. Usually he could only clearly read extremes at an initial meeting.

Like any ability of this nature, there was a wide range of talent. His youngest brothers Gage and Jack were like Diesel—they got feelings of extremes, such as love or hate, harmless or dangerous. His brother Cam could get actual words and sentences before someone spoke. So could Cam's twin, Wheeler. It was a useful skill, because often people didn't say what they were thinking. They'd thwarted a couple of robberies by being forewarned.

Axel only got images, which he said was fairly useless in the art of mind reading. During one of the robberies, he'd only seen sky and clouds in the mind of the guy holding the weapon.

Diesel suddenly realized he'd stopped talking and had simply been staring at Juliana.

She stared back with a winsome smile. He'd been woolgathering and she'd not only caught him at it, she'd remained silent and let him go off on his lengthy journey of introspection.

"What are you thinking about?" she asked.

"Nothing important. What other questions do you have for me?"

"Besides the lazy bureaucrat forefather who carelessly shortened the name Alienne to Alienn by dropping the last E, is there any other event you know of that makes people think aliens roam wild around here?" She'd mimicked his pronunciation of Alienne. Her tone of voice had some strange, goofy impact on his system and made him feel...well, a little stupid.

He pushed out a sigh. Now he needed to spout the company line about Roswell and hopefully dissuade her from following this aliens-roaming-loose track. "Back in 1947 when the incident in Roswell happened, we got a lot of attention simply because of our name. Lots of folks got all wound up, coming to Alienn from the surrounding areas to kick up a ruckus. Ultimately, nothing came of it.

"We don't have any aliens with death-ray eyes that smoke humans where they stand or a diabolical agenda to take over the planet. We just sell gas, supplies and snacks to truckers and travelers and the space theme seems to be popular with our vast and varied customers."

"So it's as simple as that. There are no aliens, the name was a typo from its inception and Maxwell the Martian is a convenient marketing mascot to sell fuel, snacks and sundries."

"Exactly."

She nodded. Her expression said she believed him, but in her mind he got a vague impression of very strong determination. But he didn't know what direction that resolve was going.

Was she satisfied with his company line or not? Had she determined that no visible hint of aliens besides Maxwell resided here, or would she be back? He hoped vigorously this wasn't the last time he'd see her. If she came back, he was fine with that. He just didn't want to fend off a publicity attack or deal with a horde of paparazzi that might accidentally discover what went on in the truck stop's basement.

"What about the cellular signal?"

"What about it?"

"Rumor has it there is not a single bar of service for nearly a ten-mile radius around Alienn and this truck stop."

"Is that a question? Sounds more like gossip."

Her eyes narrowed as if she suspected he wasn't going to cooperate with her dangerous queries.

"Okay. Why isn't there a signal for a ten-mile radius around this place?"

He shrugged. "Ask all those phone people who put up cellular towers every five feet across the land except around here. We're lucky we have hard lines so we can communicate with the outside world at all."

If Juliana ever dug deep enough, she'd find that all the strategic places where a tower could be erected to provide service in this area were owned by someone uninterested in allowing a tower to be erected at any price, ever. So far the law was on the landowner's side. If that changed, the people of Alienn would have to adapt and overcome that obstacle when the time came.

Diesel was particularly proud of the plan to

keep towers out, as he was the one who came up with it several years ago when cellular phone use was growing exponentially. He always figured it had helped him with his goal of becoming Fearless Leader. Being the oldest in his family didn't guarantee him the position. He'd had to earn it. He'd worked his butt off to get this job, truth be told. Axel had suggested there'd been a vote, but Diesel didn't think there had been. None of his brothers had wanted to be in charge. And they knew he'd wanted it more than anything else.

Juliana stared at him for several seconds before making a note on her pad. He hoped if she was able to find out why no towers had ever been allowed she'd return and ask him about it.

Juliana Masters was hands down the most beautiful woman he'd ever seen, human or Alpha.

She flipped a page, kept writing and then turned the pad over and shuffled backward through her notes. She put her pen point in the center of a random page and said, "One last thing…"

"Sure."

Her gaze lifted to his. She was gorgeous, especially her eyes. "What can you tell me about the Boogieman Affair?" she asked in a quiet voice, rocking his soul with surprise. Whoa. He hadn't seen *that* coming.

"What?" Diesel's mind raced to conjure a reasonable explanation for something that had nearly undone them, an event that until this moment he hadn't realized any earthlings had any inkling of whatsoever.

"Do I really need to repeat the question or is this a stall tactic?" Her beautiful eyebrows rose higher in challenge.

"Stall tactic," he admitted. "I hate to answer your question with a question, but—"

"I doubt that," she said under her breath.

"—where did you come by this information?"

"Is this the part where I tell you I never reveal a source?"

"I thought you were a humble writer working on an article for a book, not an investigative reporter."

"True, but I still don't have to reveal anything."

Diesel grinned. "Cool. Then neither do I."

"Oh, come on. Tell me about the Boogieman Affair."

"There's nothing to tell." Boy howdy there was *a lot* to tell, but not to any humans.

"Give me your spiel then. What's the company line?"

Diesel pushed out a sigh and recited their standard response. "It was a gas leak."

She laughed out loud. "Is that so? Does anyone still fall for that?"

He shrugged. "No comment."

"I see." She looked disappointed in him.

He felt the need to explain. "You asked for the company line and I gave it to you."

Juliana's eyes livened with unanswered questions. She was likely very dangerous, but also completely stunning. "So you admit there is more to the story?"

"No."

"You just said it was the company line."

"That doesn't mean it isn't true." *Liar, liar, pants on fire.*

"Of course it does. That's what *company line* means. It is the lie the public is told to keep them in the dark about what really goes on to protect our delicate sensibilities."

"Or it's the truth and nothing important happened." He threw his hands up, feigning exasperation to help sell his point. "We just sell fuel and snacks. How does that translate into some dark conspiracy?"

"What made you say the words 'dark conspiracy'? *Is* there a dark conspiracy here in Alienn? Is that what the Boogieman Affair was?"

"No." *There is a light conspiracy gently cascading over all the area and there has been for several decades, with a singular dark incident in the recent past that I choose not to explain.*

"Really?" Her tone dripped with sarcasm.

"There is no dark conspiracy," he insisted. *It's totally a conspiracy and a very dark incident I can never share with you, no matter how pretty you are.*

"So you say the 'Boogieman Affair' was nothing, but you also said the company line stated it was a gas leak."

"Yes. So what?"

"Well, isn't gas leaking a rather important incident?"

"What are you really asking me?"

"There were rumors of a dark entity skulking through town and part of the truck stop, causing mischief and mayhem to anyone or anything it encountered. First of all, it doesn't sound like a gas leak kind of incident. Second of all, a gas leak? Really? It's kind of cliché as an explanation, if you ask me."

"Luckily, I didn't ask you." Diesel frowned. He didn't mean to be so terse, but only the extraterrestrial residents of Alienn had been privy to the events of that dark night and, truthfully, not all of *them* were fully apprised of every detail in that matter. And absolutely no humans had been told anything. "Who have you been talking to about this...incident?"

She put her fingers up to her lips, made the universal tick-a-lock gesture and threw away an imaginary key.

He focused on her face, specifically, her beautiful eyes. He stared deeply, trying to search her mind for the information he sought. The only message he received was the seemingly very strong and growing attraction she felt for him.

Diesel wasn't certain if he'd projected it or if she was projecting it or if they were trading projections of wild attraction, though he suddenly rooted for option number three. Mutual wild attraction with a beautiful human was certainly an unexpected part of his day. It had never happened before.

He didn't see anything else in her mind. No hint of where she'd come by this privy information about a dark incident in Alienn's recent past, simply her interest in him and her appreciation for his appearance, which had surprised her, too.

"What do you see in my mind?" she asked quietly.

"You like me," he said without thinking how odd the question was coming from a human, then added, "And you also think I'm very attractive." In for a penny, in for a pound, he always said.

The blush that bloomed in her cheeks was fast and furious. It was then he noticed how close they stood together. He bent his head nearer to her face and her lips, breathing in her luscious scent. Their mouths were mere inches apart.

Were they about to kiss? He paused, not moving forward to connect.

She whispered, "Do you truly believe that you can romance me and get me to stop asking questions? You are very handsome, which I suspect you already know, but I have an article to complete so I can earn a rather large bonus for my future. It is very important to me. Therefore, I won't be put off so easily."

Diesel straightened to his full height, breaking any magical connection they'd shared and ignoring the implication that he was conceited about his looks. He was being ridiculous. She was here for a specific purpose, one he needed to subdue. He was projecting his personal feelings in her direction, because he'd read in her mind that she thought he was attractive and he felt the same way about her. Merely shaking hands with her had created a spark. Sure. It could merely be static in the air, but what if it was more?

As Diesel stared into her eyes, vague impressions started flowing into his mind to the point he was certain she was thinking the words, *Kiss me. Kiss me. Kiss me.*

No good could come of any further connection—romantic, spark-filled or otherwise—with this beautiful earthling. Especially not kissing her.

It took all the willpower he possessed not to lower his mouth to hers—*it would be so easy*—and discover what she tasted like, but the mental image of doing just that wouldn't fade. He bent forward again, against his better judgement, losing the already weak willpower battle.

He needed to stop.

He needed to get a grip.

He needed to send her on her way.

He stared at her mouth.

He needed to kiss her.

Diesel pressed his lips to hers before rational thought could stop him. He justified the move with the idea he was merely diverting her from questions he didn't want to answer to checking out their physical compatibility with a kiss.

Juliana's lips were soft and pliable and she didn't discourage him as he half expected. In fact, she kissed him right back rather ardently. They seemed *very* compatible. She was the most compatible female he'd ever touched. And truthfully, this was the first fully involved romantic kiss he'd ever shared with a human, and it was awesome.

Diesel needed to stop kissing her, but knew he didn't have the desire, the willpower or the fortitude to break from this most alluring connection.

Juliana wanted Diesel to kiss her so desperately; she figured if he was reading her mind, he'd see her seductive longing and possibly fulfill her avid wishes. *Kiss me, kiss me, kiss me.*

And he had.

And the kiss was so amazingly good.

And she wanted it to last forever.

If it hadn't been for someone nearby clearing their throat very loudly—several moments after their mouths connected—who knows how long they would have kept up the delicious lip lock? Would he have dragged her into a janitor's closet to have his wicked, possibly alien, way with her? She hadn't noticed one in this hallway, only the two bathrooms.

Maybe he would have pulled her toward his office, pushed her down on his receptionist's perfectly ordered desk to enact his wild, alien plan to seduce her? Would she have let him? That was unclear, but it was very likely given her very un-Juliana-like actions up to this point.

"Sorry to interrupt," said a male voice to her left after the throat-clearing didn't separate them. "But I need to have a word with you."

Diesel lifted his head. "What is it, Axel?" he asked curtly.

"Come back into your office, O Fearless Leader, and I'll tell you everything."

Diesel rolled his eyes and then met Julian's gaze. He smiled, winked and whispered, "My brother, whom I will yell at for the interruption, apparently needs a word. I'll be right back to walk you out to your car. Okay?"

Juliana couldn't speak yet so she nodded, trying to remember how to breathe after that amazing kiss. She wanted to stay and ask more questions; maybe other scandalous queries might cause him to kiss her again in an effort to keep her quiet. A strangely giddy feeling rose up inside her the moment Diesel was out of sight. She couldn't wait until he got back. Was this what love at first sight felt like?

Juliana hadn't ever had much of a romantic life to speak of. Not like the girls she'd gone to school with who never went more than a few days between boyfriends, as if being alone was the more hideous choice than being in a loud, caustic shouting match of a relationship, continually spiraling down an emotional drain.

Sure, she'd dated on occasion. She'd even had a boyfriend for a short time, but if she was honest, many of her dates in the last year or two had been blind dates thrust on her by well-meaning friends who felt sorry for her lack of day-to-day male companionship.

As far as men she'd personally shown any interested in, there were very few of them. They all had ended up being a disappointment in one way or another.

Maybe she was too picky. Maybe she was afraid of getting hurt. Maybe she didn't want the drama that so many relationships eventually devolved into, a sight she'd witnessed too many times to count.

Then again, if any man had ever kissed her like Diesel had, she might have reconsidered. No kiss before today had ever lit her up inside and radiated outward as it progressed. That kiss had definitely been worthy of her time and attention.

As she waited for Diesel to come back, Juliana contemplated the walk to her car. Would he kiss her again? Maybe she would kiss him this time.

Maybe she wanted to ensure the delicious sensation wasn't unique to the first kiss. Maybe a second kiss would yield nothing, no spark whatsoever. But she seriously doubted it.

Or maybe this was the start of something wonderful. Finally and at long last she'd have a boyfriend she selected, one who made her happy and alive with a mere brush of his lips on hers. Not to mention that he had some family or at least a brother named Axel, prompting her next thought about the Grey brothers' interesting names. Diesel and Axel? Well, they did work at a truck stop.

Juliana was all alone in the world, a nameless orphan left on a church doorstep when she was less than a year old. Named for a 4th century saint by the nuns at the church, well, the feminized version, anyway. Juliana's last name, Masters, was also invented, possibly from a lock manufacturer in Milwaukee, and altered slightly, but that hadn't ever been verified. She couldn't even investigate where she'd come from since no one had a clue as to her true origin. No parents. No grandparents. No aunts, uncles or cousins. No one. Nothing special left with her to indicate where on earth she'd come from. Not a single, solitary clue.

The seeming hopelessness of discovering her origins didn't thwart her desire to try, though. She planned to travel to the city she'd been found in just as soon as she had enough money to do so. She wanted to make an effort to discover why she'd been left at a church.

She'd been abandoned in a port city in the Northwest. At eighteen, a full-ride scholarship to a college in Missouri brought her to the center of the country. After graduating with honors, she accepted a second scholarship to graduate school in Arkansas. The life she carved out for herself had been achieved with hard work and the fortitude to never settle for less than her very best effort.

Her goals were simple. She wanted to travel. She wanted to work hard at a job she enjoyed. She wanted to find someone she loved to share her life with and, most important of all, she wanted to have a big family with lots of kids.

One guy she'd dated for a very short time during her first year of college had mentioned in passing his distaste for children. She'd broken up with him soon after. He'd been stunned. He even tried to persuade her to stay in the relationship by telling her there were already too many children in the world and they could travel so much easier without "curtain climbers" sucking the resources out of their lives.

She never spoke to him again.

A rogue thought intruded. What if Diesel doesn't want kids? *Please want kids. Please want kids.* She'd have to ask as soon as he returned. Regardless of his ability to bestow amazing kisses, he had to want kids someday or she'd immediately stop fantasizing about a romantic life with him.

Diesel appeared in the hallway as if conjured by her saddened feelings about possibly putting a stop to whatever was happening between them before any further kissing took place.

"Something wrong?" he asked as he approached. He put a hand on her shoulder as if to comfort her. Even his platonic touch warmed her all the way to her bones.

Juliana perked up the moment she felt his warmth. "No. I guess not." *All isn't lost, at least not yet.*

"Are you sure?" His brows furrowed as if he truly worried about her. *Do I look that forlorn?* Abruptly he asked, "Do you have more questions?"

"Yes. Do you ever want to have children?"

"I beg your pardon?" Perhaps he'd been expecting more questions about the Boogieman Affair. Or the strange goings on in and around Alienn. It didn't matter. More than anything else in the moment, she wanted to know if there was any kind of future to their relationship.

"It's a simple question. Kids. Do you want them? Yes or no." Juliana didn't mean to sound so belligerent, but she suddenly and truly needed to know his exact feelings on a future family.

He nodded. "Someday…with the right person." He looked deeply into her eyes. "Sure. I do want children. I have a large family so—"

"Really," she broke in. "How many kids in your family?"

"Seven."

"Seven! That's awesome." Juliana was delighted. This was the best news ever. Diesel was perfect. He warmed her from head to toe with a mere look. He kissed like a dream. He came from a large family and, best of all, he wanted kids. Did he want *seven* kids? She'd always wanted four, but she could certainly be persuaded to have more.

"I'm so glad you appreciate my large family. Here, let me walk you to your car," he said, his tone conveyed uncertainty. Understandable, given that she was acting like an infatuated idiot and they'd met less than thirty minutes ago. He gestured toward the hallway and a door that said, "Employees Only."

"Am I allowed through here?"

"Well, I *am* the Fearless Leader, after all. Seems like I should be able to go out any door I want to with any guest I choose. Right?"

"Sure. Let's go with that." She smiled and walked forward, her mind swirling at the possibility of a huge family in her future with Diesel. She'd never believed in love at first sight, but felt like she was experiencing it firsthand. She fairly floated down the hallway to the outside door.

They remained silent as they exited the building. He'd promised to walk her to her vehicle. Perhaps she could convince him to kiss her again. A dreamy goodbye kiss she could think about on her way home.

Her attention was drawn to movement on her right. She looked and saw something unexpected. She stared at something she couldn't quite understand. Something she couldn't explain. Something...not of this world. It wasn't slimy or three-eyed, but it was also definitely not human. It was like a man on the bottom and a sea creature on top, complete with eight tentacles floating around his body. Was she dreaming? Was she crazy?

She turned toward Diesel and heard him curse under his breath. Oh no.

Was this a horrifying reboot of the Boogieman Affair? Was she about to become another victim of a disavowed dark conspiracy?

Chapter 4

As Diesel shepherded Juliana out through the employees-only door, he pondered the information Axel had given him, wondering why his brother had needed to take even five minutes to discuss what they'd already talked about regarding the new prison run deal. The transports would come at the first of the month, every month, even if they didn't have prisoners on board because they also carried supplies from Alpha-Prime and retrieved prisoner-made items created during scheduled work time. Mostly lots of pea gravel, but occasionally artists and craftsmen were confined.

Axel especially wanted to take advantage of the special addendum option on the contract Diesel had just signed. The monthly stops would be the bread and butter of the deal, but the special runs could prove very lucrative. The ink on the deal wasn't even dry yet and Axel had found an unscheduled run they could take on for their first use of the contract. He wanted Diesel's okay for what he called, "A small trial run of this contract."

Only three people would be on the ship headed for the gulag: the pilot, the guard and one prisoner.

Axel felt it was a perfect test.

Diesel didn't really care when UGG started running prison ships to Earth or how many occupants would be visiting. He'd already signed the paper without discussing it with the home planet or the council. It was his call on both counts anyway. Letting Alpha-Prime and the council of elders know about the contract was simply a courtesy on his part, tradition, because that's the way it had always been done.

The entire time he'd been speaking with Axel, his mind had been on Juliana and the kiss and how he wanted to do it again. Maybe he could kiss her goodbye and then invite her back for a real date?

"So what do you think?"

He almost said, "About the kiss?" He stopped himself in time. "Fine. Whatever. Let's talk about it later, okay?"

He headed back down the hallway, past the bathrooms toward the Maxwell the Martian booth, worried the whole way that she wouldn't be waiting for him.

She was exactly where he'd left her.

He was surprised by her direct questions about kids and family, but maybe it was a human thing he'd never encountered before. Reluctantly, he led her to the employees-only door. He was an employee. Although he usually gave anyone else who worked in the truck stop endless grief for allowing civilians through the door, he was the Fearless Leader and he could mostly do what he wanted. Besides, he was escorting someone out, not sneaking someone into the building.

Outside, they'd have more privacy. Maybe he would have the opportunity to get an extra kiss goodbye and he'd definitely ask her to come back. Or out on a date.

If she didn't want to return to the truck stop, perhaps on his day off he could visit her wherever she lived. Crazy, because he rarely left town on his day off. In fact, he rarely even *took* a day off.

She'd been so excited to discover he had a huge family. Others were not so excited about that information and had looked down their noses at the idea of seven children. Juliana had been animated, excited and happy that he came from a large family, and that fact briefly stunned his senses. His focus was completely on her and not their current surroundings as he ushered Juliana out the employees-only door into the usually empty side alley. That was a mistake. A big one.

The moment he stepped onto the cement slab leading to the parking lot and the door closed with finality behind him, he looked up and saw a huge, inescapable problem.

The emergency basement doors leading to the underground facility that housed all their clandestine alien everything were standing wide open about thirty feet away. What the hell!

A Moogallian was just about to go down the stairs. The tourist lifted four of its eight tentacles, emitted a high, piercing scream and promptly fell down into a heap, apparently fainting at its first sight of a human.

What incredibly imperfect timing.

Juliana turned to Diesel with eyes as wide as the full moon scheduled for two nights from now. "You saw that, right?"

Diesel didn't answer. He just stood there wondering what in the world he was going to do now. He knew what he *should* do. He inhaled to explain, unsure of even what words would come out of his mouth courtesy of his flash-stunned brain.

He put an arm around her as she pointed at the being lying prostrate at the opening of their secret basement alien bunker leading into questions he absolutely could not answer.

"Please tell me you saw that," she repeated in a quivery, frightened voice.

"Better not."

Before he could say anything else—and his mind was blank as to any content—he caught movement out of the corner of his eye over her shoulder and his attention was drawn from her stunned expression to yet another potential problem. *Now what?*

Diesel recognized his brother, Cam, approaching at a fast clip. Relief rushed through his body.

Cam was in charge of security for not only the truck stop but also the secret underground bunker. He'd know what to do in this situation. He'd take care of this issue pronto.

"Hey, Cam," Diesel said, hoping Juliana would also look away from the motionless visitor from Moogally who decorated the ground by the open basement doors.

"Juliana, this is my brother, Cam," Diesel dutifully introduced them.

She turned away from the fainting alien problem and looked straight at his brother. Cam glanced in her direction, gave Diesel a stern, disapproving frown, lifted his arm from his side and aimed a Defender at Juliana.

"Don't shoot her!" Diesel said, then, "You shot her." He couldn't believe it. How could Cam be so callous?

Juliana slumped against Diesel, unconscious. He caught her before she hit the ground. Sliding one arm behind her back and another beneath her legs, he lifted her limp body against his and prepared to have a big fat fight with Cam. "What did you do that for?"

"Security."

Diesel glanced at the Defender. "I hate it when you use that thing." A weapon that rendered humans unconscious and affected their memories, it was only supposed to be used in very limited and extreme cases.

"And I hate it that you don't use it enough."

"I'm not a *blast first, ask questions later* kind of guy, since we definitely can't get any answers now." Diesel hugged Juliana closer, trying not to despair.

"I know, but that's what you pay me to do. She was here to ask about whether aliens lived among us, spouted information about the Boogieman Affair and we certainly didn't need to let her leave with positive proof from Mr. Drunken Moogallian over there."

"How do you know why Juliana was here?"

"It's my job to know."

Diesel resisted the desire to grunt in frustration. Cam was right, but he didn't have to like it. He looked down at Juliana's limp form. Eyes closed, she was still the most beautiful woman he'd ever seen. A more alarming thought occurred to him. What memories had been lost with that irreversible blast from the Defender? The last five minutes? More?

"What was the Defender set on, Cam?" he asked, uncertain he wanted to know the answer. "Tell me it was only five minutes."

His brother looked at the top of the device to check, brows lifting in what looked like surprise. "It's set on the maximum," he said in a self-satisfied tone.

Diesel's jaw muscles clenched until he feared he'd crack a tooth. He moved his jaw from side to side before speaking. "It was unnecessary to use the maximum setting, Cam. I could have handled the situation without use of the Defender."

"Except that I'm the one charged with ensuring humans don't discover our existence here. I'm the one who decides when and how much force is needed to suppress humans from finding out the truth."

"All I'm saying is that you didn't have to erase her memory for thirty minutes. She hasn't even been here at the truck stop that long." If he'd set the Defender for only five minutes, Diesel could have taken her back inside the convenience store, parked her in the reception area and that would have kept her from remembering the non-humanoid alien she'd seen.

Cam shot a quick look at his wristwatch and shrugged. "She's been here for twenty-six minutes. Close enough."

Diesel glared at Cam. "So rounding up, it's thirty?"

"Yes. It *is* close enough. What is the problem? Put the human in her car and she can try again. This time don't take her out the employee door. That was foolish, Diesel."

Diesel ignored the dig and said, "I don't know which car is hers."

"I do."

"How do you know? Were you watching her?"

"Of course I was watching her. I saw her arrive. Have I ever mentioned that I take my job in security very seriously? Speaking of which, have you changed your passwords lately?"

Diesel lifted the beautiful Juliana a little higher in his arms and tightened his hold as he frowned at his brother. He was in no mood to discuss password safety and his brother's endless and overbearing precautions. He negotiated the tall wooden gate next to the store with Cam's help and crossed into the public parking area. "Which car is hers?"

Cam pointed to a small silver-gray sedan. "That one."

They looked around to see who might be watching them. It was a quiet evening, shockingly enough. She'd parked out of direct sight of the gas pumps and hopefully no one could see Diesel holding the unconscious Juliana.

Diesel carried her to the car and pulled the driver's door handle. Locked. He again looked around to ensure he was alone and shuffled her in his arms until her head rested on his shoulder and the rest of her limp body was secured only by one arm around her waist.

Cam joined him. "Hurry and get her in there. Someone's bound to come by or she's going to wake up."

Diesel stepped away from the vehicle. "Then help me unlock her door."

Cam rifled through her purse without remorse. He retrieved her keys, opened the door, put the key in the ignition and stepped back. Diesel carefully placed her in the seat behind the wheel, put her seat belt on and arranged her so she wouldn't slump over. He smoothed her hair away from her lovely face as Cam whispered, fiercely, "She's fine. Let's go."

They shut her door and backed away from the vehicle. Diesel hated to leave her unattended.

"You can't be here when she wakes up."

"I know that, but nothing better happen to her before she comes to. Keep an eye on her."

Cam gave him a narrow-eyed look. "She's a human." His tone suggested it wasn't important to worry about what might happen to a human who'd been zapped with a Big D.

"I'm aware."

The flinty gaze continued. "What is she to you?"

The first human I've ever kissed. And I liked it. A lot. While Alphas could sometimes read human minds, the same could not be said about each other. Luckily, Diesel's memories were his alone to ponder and revisit.

"She is someone who came in to ask me for information about Alienn, Arkansas and how it came to be named that and why there's no cellular service. She's doing some sort of article for a travel book. I gave her the standard spiel."

They'd made it out of view of Juliana's vehicle.

Cam crossed his arms. "The standard spiel? Tell me exactly what you said to her."

"I thought you saw the surveillance."

"I saw part of it. I didn't memorize it. Yet."

"I told her that Alienn was supposed to be named Alienne after a woman who founded the town long ago and not an indication of extraterrestrial life here on Earth. And that a lazy bureaucrat put Alienn in the paperwork, dropping the final E, and that it stuck, and also the 'ask the phone tower people about the lack of a signal here' spiel."

Cam looked dubious. "And did she believe you?"

"I don't know. Octo-alien with the scaredy-cat squeal came out of nowhere and fainted at the emergency basement exit—which should not have been open, by the way—and then you shot her in the face with the Big D."

Cam's mouth flattened. "And here's something funny and unexpected—you have been rather protective of this human since she arrived."

Diesel looked over his shoulder in the direction of Juliana's car. "I don't want anything to happen to her because of what you did."

"I had to do it. You know I did. You're acting like a mama bear that had her cubs stolen. What's that about?"

"Maybe, I don't like that it complicates things. Why couldn't you set it for five minutes instead of forever?"

"It was hardly forever. It was only thirty minutes, which is the longest setting. Tell me the truth, Diesel. What is your interest in this human?"

"None of your business."

"But it *is* my business."

"Fine. I like her."

"Why?"

"I just do."

Cam made a face. "Wait a minute. You're promised to a woman on Alpha-Prime."

"No."

"Yes, you are."

"The contract says it has to be one of us. Doesn't mean it has to be me. You know the eldest often is excluded because he gets stuck with everything else. Like being the Fearless Leader of the Big Bang Truck Stop for our Earth-bound lifelong career."

Cam shook his head, frowning as if trying to remember the specifics of the marriage that had been arranged for one of the Grey sons before any of them had been born. "No. I think it's the eldest who needs a bride to carry on the family name. Also, mating with indigenous people and producing Alpha-human hybrids for a future generation isn't typically allowed, even if you weren't promised."

"That's not true. Besides, there are six of us men in the family. Only one of us has to fulfill that arranged marriage proxy. And even *that* arrangement is not set to go into effect for quite a while yet."

Cam tempered his harsh visage. "Are you soft for this human, Diesel?"

"What?"

"You heard me."

"Soft isn't the word I'd use. I like her. She's smart. She makes me feel different. She makes me feel good."

"Because she thinks you're attractive."

Diesel gave Cam a long, hard stare. "How do you know that?"

Cam huffed. "I'm in security. I'll refer you back to the surveillance images I saw earlier."

"How do you know she thinks I'm attractive, Cam?"

"Axel wasn't the only one who saw you kiss her, Diesel. I have it recorded on the store security logs. Would you like a copy of it, perhaps?" he asked sarcastically.

Juliana opened her eyes, confused by her familiar-yet-unfamiliar surroundings, then realized she must have fallen asleep in her car. Yes, it had been a long day. Yes, she was tired. No, she'd never dozed off in her car before. She didn't even remember parking here. She shook off the remnants of her lethargy and grabbed her keys from the ignition, thankful she'd at least had the wherewithal to turn her car off before her unexpected nap.

On the drive here, she'd been thinking about what might happen when she broached the question about aliens running wild on planet Earth, especially in this particular area of Arkansas.

She got out of her car slowly, feeling a strange sense of déjà vu when she walked toward the convenience store. She'd never been here before, to the best of her knowledge. Maybe all truck stops looked alike.

Her initial probable scenario about this coming conversation involved meeting a short, rotund man in a silver lamé costume who smoked a cigar and stared at her legs. But all of a sudden a completely different scenario slid into her mind with a vivid yet dreamlike quality she'd never experienced before.

What if the manager of this place was tall, dark and handsome? No, tall, *fair* and handsome. What if he mesmerized her with his blue-eyed gaze and kissed her to make her forget why she came here? A buzzing feeling settled in her belly, slowing her steps as she created a vision of what an alien kiss might be like. It would be amazing. Wait. *How do I know that?*

Juliana almost stopped walking before she shook off the foolish notion, picked up her pace and headed inside the convenience store portion of the Big Bang Truck Stop. It was already full dark outside. How long had she been asleep? A glance at her watch told her she'd napped for almost half an hour. She shook her head and reconsidered starting a vitamin regimen.

She was certain she'd never been here before, but the clerk looked familiar for some reason. He had straight black hair, dark caramel skin and a diamond stud in one earlobe. The silver lamé uniform looked good on him. His nametag said, "Welcome, Earthling! My name is Paulo." He started to smile, and Juliana knew he had perfect white teeth before he opened his mouth. *How do I know* that?

Paulo grinned and nodded, proving out her prediction of perfectly straight white teeth. So what? Lots of people have white teeth. Yes. True. But the feeling in her gut said she'd seen his smile before. *How is that possible?* She'd never been here before.

Juliana shook off her vague discomfort and asked, "Hi. Could you direct me to where I could speak to the manager of this place?" *He's going to point you to the back corner of the building and tell you to ask for…*what was the name of the manager? Gasoline…color. No. *What is the name?* It was on the tip of her tongue.

"He's right over there." Paulo turned and pointed toward two men standing ten feet away. They seemed to be having a curt, unhappy discussion. Juliana thanked the clerk and approached the two men, feeling quite a bit off balance and hating to interrupt an argument.

The taller of the two men glanced in her direction as she approached and gave her a smile. Whew! He was attractive. He had dark blond hair, vivid blue eyes, a five o'clock shadow covering his solid jaw and chin, plus a wide, engaging smile that almost made her forget her own name. She looked down at his chest, noting he wasn't wearing silver lamé or a nametag like Paulo.

The other man looked similar in coloring, but had a frown on his face. A deeper grimace registered when he glanced over his shoulder and saw her.

Juliana extended her hand to the very attractive man and said, "Hi, I'm Juliana Masters. Are you the manager of this place?" Without letting him answer, because she knew he was in charge, she quickly said, "I wondered if I might have a few minutes of your time to help me with an article I'm doing for a special new Finder's book."

Mr. Scowl Face extended his hand in her direction. "I'm the one in charge. What is it you need?"

"No, you're not," she said, returning his scowl. She looked at the other man—the very attractive one—and said, "He's Diesel Grey and he's in charge here." *How do I know his name? Did Mr. Harriman tell me that? Maybe.*

Before she could ponder how she knew his name or why she got the strong feeling they'd met before, the deeply delicious-looking man extended his hand. "Yes. That's right. I am the manager here. This is my brother, Cam. He's in charge of security."

Cam huffed and took a step back. "This discussion isn't over, Diesel. Come find me once you answer her…questions." He pointed at the front door of the store where she'd just come in. "And by the way, *that's* the exit."

Juliana expected him to add, "Don't let the door hit you in the ass on your way out." But he didn't. He just gave his brother a stern look and walked away.

"Did I say something wrong?" she asked.

"No. Don't mind him. He's just having a bad day. He shouldn't take it out on others." Diesel put his full attention on her. "What can I help you with, Juliana?" *Say my name again. I like your voice.*

Juliana felt heat rise in her cheeks. She stared at him just a little too long after his question, deciding he was certainly more attractive than she'd initially pictured. "I wanted to ask about the rumors surrounding Alienn, Arkansas and this truck stop."

"Rumors?" he asked, clearly amused. "Like are there really aliens living in the area?"

Her eyes narrowed. "Yes. How did you guess?"

He lifted one muscled shoulder in a shrug. "Do you know how many people come here to ask me that on a day-to-day basis?"

Juliana couldn't seem to stop staring. "Are you really going to answer my question with a question?" The hair on the back of her neck stood up as she asked the question. She felt like this conversation was familiar, but not quite right.

Diesel brushed two fingers along his temple then suddenly wiped his palm from forehead to chin as if to reject whatever he'd wanted to say in order to say something less inflammatory. He looked over one shoulder briefly before turning back to her. She looked in the same direction, but only saw the in-store security camera mounted up in the corner.

"So, how about it? Will you answer my questions?"

He gestured to the front door. Was he kicking her out? "Why don't we talk outside?"

Juliana narrowed her eyes. "Don't you have an office or something?"

"Or something and it's a mess. It's a nice evening. Why don't we take a stroll outside instead?"

Feeling a bit like she was being shuffled out to be dismissed, Juliana turned and walked slowly back the way she'd come. Diesel stepped in front of her, put his large warm hand on the center of her back and pushed the swinging glass door open to let her go through first.

She shivered the moment he touched her as if he held some manner of sway over her soul. The distinct desire to kiss him and discover what he tasted like rose in her vivid imagination like a boogieman ready to strike her down if she didn't make a concerted effort to act on her instinct and find out. What was that all about?

His palm still touching her back, Diesel ushered her several steps into the mostly empty parking lot, stopping at the corner nearest the side lot where her car was parked. The scent of gasoline wafted past her nose, not surprisingly, since the station's vast array of pumps were within view.

Diesel's hand dropped from her back and she missed the connection instantly. "Okay, now that we're all alone out here, what's the standard company line that you give out when hordes of people ask about alien activity in the area or why the town is named Alienn?"

He stared at her, gazing intently into her eyes, with his arms crossed over his chest and a familiar smile shaping his luscious mouth, a mouth that she wanted to taste again. Wait. Taste again? No, she hadn't tasted him yet. *But you want to.* Yes, that was certainly true.

Juliana was unprepared for him to move closer. He bent forward a bit and she mentally measured the distance between their lips, wishing he'd make it easier for her to reach him. "The standard company line regarding the town's name has to do with a lazy bureaucrat who wrote Alienn on the town's papers of incorporation, dropping the last E, instead of the female founder's name, which was Alienne." He pronounced it *I-lean,* and then he spelled the name for her. She loved his Arkansas-flavored Southern accent, even when he spelled.

"I see." He smelled so good, he was so attractive and his voice was soothing and exciting all at the same time. "What about the aliens possibly running around in the area?"

He shrugged. "Do you see any?"

The image of a half octopus-half man appeared briefly in her mind. She shook it off, deciding it must have been a creature from some late-night movie marathon she'd half slept through.

Juliana glanced around the area but only saw people pumping gas or shopping in the convenience store. A look the other way showed the Cosmos Café with a fair number of customers and the Satellite Truck Wash. Next to the truck wash was the Black Hole Movie Theater. No out-of-place aliens in sight.

She looked back at Diesel and had the most powerful feeling they'd met before.

"What about the lack of cellular service in the area?"

"You'd have to ask the people who put the towers up. Perhaps we've angered them somehow and now we're being punished with a lack of cellular service."

Juliana watched his mouth the whole time he spoke. The answer he gave was expected, but the desire to kiss him was…well…alien to her. A smile formed on his mouth and she started to ask if they'd ever crossed paths, but she got fixated on the shape of his lips. Would they be firm or soft? Firm, surely. What would he taste like? Would his kiss knock her socks off? Did she want to find out? She knew his kiss would be the best she'd ever had in her life. Wait.

How do I know that?

"Is that all? Are you satisfied?" he asked, not moving away as she basically stared at him. Her gaze fixed on his engaging blue eyes. His sexy half-smile undid her. *Am I satisfied?*

"No," she said quickly. "I'm nowhere near satisfied." Juliana closed the distance between them, lifted up on her toes and planted her mouth on his, kissing him like she wanted to devour him. Her hands steadied on his biceps. He was so warm.

The kiss she'd wanted since the first second she'd seen him was everything she expected and more. The kiss was as amazing as she'd imagined it would be. His lips were firm, memorable and comfortable territory.

Wait.

Why did their first kiss seem so…familiar?

Chapter 5

Diesel couldn't believe she'd kissed him. But he intended to enjoy it. He relaxed into her open arms, sliding his hands around her waist, pressing his fingertips into the muscle along either side of her spine as the sultry lip lock continued and then deepened.

After a long and invigorating kiss, Juliana broke away. Diesel released her waist. She sucked in a breath, put the tips of her fingers to her lips as if they'd been burned and stared at him in wonder. Her mouth opened and closed as if she didn't know what to say. The kiss had been as amazing as their first one. But from this day forward, he'd have to remember *this* had been their first kiss from her current perspective.

"*Now* are you satisfied?" he asked. He grinned so she'd understand he wasn't upset about the kiss.

"Yes. Quite." She didn't smile back. She looked a bit dazed. For him, the kiss had been even better than their first.

Juliana took a step back and looked toward her

car. Her cheeks blazed bright with color. Without looking at him, she said, "I'm sorry to have been so forward. I don't know what came over me." Her expression wasn't contrite, since she was basically grinning. She seemed happy she'd done it, but confused.

"That's okay. It wasn't a trial, trust me."

She turned toward him and pulled out her steno pad. He panicked for a moment. Hadn't she taken notes earlier? Using the Defender was difficult in some circumstances. Diesel's mind traipsed back over the thirty minutes she'd lost—or rather, the twenty-six minutes with her he'd never get back. It was a crime of nature as far as he was concerned. But often he didn't get to decide his own best interests.

She seemed distracted, but apparently her notebook wasn't a concern.

"What's wrong?" he asked.

Juliana's sultry, intense gaze came up, shooting a look directly into his eyes. He was mesmerized.

"That kiss..." she said quietly, not finishing the thought. Her eyes narrowed. "It felt comfortable. No. That's not right." She stared at him again. "It felt familiar. Have we ever met before?"

Diesel felt his eyes widen. She couldn't possibly remember. "That's not what you mean, is it? You're asking if we've ever kissed before." *Space potatoes! What am I saying?*

She brightened all of a sudden and a beautiful

smile surfaced. She shook her head again. "I know. It's crazy. Never mind. I'm a little off my game for some reason." She glanced back at her car for a minute and he wondered if she remembered her "nap."

He felt the need to distract her. He put a hand on her soft shoulder briefly to gain her attention. "I'm certain that I'd recollect if we had ever kissed before." *It was amazing that first time. I regret only that it was erased from your memory.*

Juliana nodded. "I agree. Hard to forget something like that." Her expression softened and her gaze moved over his shoulder as if her memory went off into the distance trying to recapture a dream.

The Defender removed all human memories for the selected time period as if they'd never occurred. No remembering as if it were a dream. No déjà vu moments where the human thought they'd been here before or experienced something before. The Defender eliminated the memory completely within the prescribed time frame. Always. Without fail.

Luckily it only worked on humans and had no effect on the alien population on Earth. She couldn't possibly remember anything. So why did it seem like she was remembering their first kiss?

He didn't know exactly where Cam had placed each and every camera he monitored, just that he was somewhere watching, likely waiting to argue with Diesel over the second kiss. But Diesel didn't regret it. Besides, he hadn't instigated it. She had. What did Cam expect him to do? Push her away in disgust? Not a chance.

"Do you have any more questions?" he asked abruptly, thinking about the coming difficult conversation with Cam. There would be a lecture from his security-minded brother to annoy him, even as on some remote level he knew Cam was right about this.

Juliana startled, looked down at her steno pad, flipped a page up, studied it and then looked at him. She glanced back down at her page again, as if contemplating what she wanted to say. Her mouth quirked up on one side. She was obviously wrestling with something. Then he remembered the conversation they'd been having about something a human shouldn't have known about. Had Cam heard her mention the Boogieman Affair earlier? Since his brother hadn't castigated him for that yet, Diesel could probably look forward to it next time.

She lowered the page. "I guess that's all I have for now, but I wonder if we could meet again."

"Meet? Again?" he said stupidly, as part of his mind warred with how seeing her again was probably not a good idea at the same time he wanted to make a date with her more than anything. Diesel would meet with her anywhere, anytime.

Juliana tapped her notebook with the end of her

pen once. "Yes. Maybe when you aren't working."
I'm always working.

"Sure," he said. "When did you have in mind?"

"When is your next day off?" *I don't get days off.*

"I'm the boss. I can take off whenever I like." *I'm so funny.*

She smiled. "Okay. How about next Friday then? I'm free that day."

Diesel knew Friday was a bad day for her to be at the truck stop. "What if I come to you this time? Then there won't be a chance of us getting interrupted with my job, because the truth is, whenever I'm here, I'm working."

Her beautiful smile lit up her face. "Perfect." She ripped a blank piece of paper out of her steno pad and started writing. "Here is my address. I have a small apartment just off campus, in Doraydo. And I'll also put my cell phone number down." She stopped writing and her gaze found his, giving him an intensely gratifying stare. "You know, in case you need to call me before Friday."

"What time on Friday would you like to meet?" He glanced at the address and number she'd written down to memorize them before folding the paper to shove in his front pocket.

"I could make us some lunch. So how about around eleven o'clock?"

"Great. I'll be there." Diesel took a step backward, knowing that if he stayed close, smelling her scent, he might kiss her again.

She looked down and then retreated toward her car, taking a small step in that direction. "I'll see you in a few days then."

"Yes."

"Thank you for your time."

"Sure."

Juliana got into her car, started it up and backed out of the parking space. Diesel didn't exhale until she drove out of the truck stop parking lot. He stood there for several minutes watching her car merge onto the surprisingly light Route 88 traffic headed west toward Doraydo, a nearby college town.

Wait until he mentioned to anyone in his family that he was taking Friday off to visit a human in another town. *She lives in Doraydo, less than an hour away.* That news would certainly generate some wild speculation and fuel the truck stop gossip mill for weeks to come.

Even the idea of being the fodder for gossip didn't stop Diesel from looking forward to seeing Juliana again.

Juliana drove home as if in a trance. She didn't remember arriving at the Big Bang Truck Stop and she barely remembered the drive back to her place. What she did remember, vividly, was kissing Diesel Grey. That moment played over and over in her mind all the way back to Doraydo.

Before she knew it she was a mile away from pulling into her apartment parking lot, marveling at her lack of awareness during both the trip to Alienn and the return journey. Not to mention the surprise nap she'd taken before even going inside the truck stop's convenience store to inquire about speaking to the manager.

The boringly named College Apartments sign and turn-off came up soon enough. She steered her car into the lot and drove slowly toward her assigned space. She'd been lucky to find this place.

The apartment she had lived in since moving to Arkansas was a bit older, but also very clean and the neighbors were friendly. The ones she saw, anyway. She'd renewed the lease after graduation because a quick search around town yielded nothing else she could afford.

Besides, it would be difficult to leave Miss Penny behind.

Her neighbor across the hall was quite a pistol, but she was also a good soul. No matter what time of the day or night Juliana returned to her apartment, Miss Penny would stick her head out and offer a greeting.

Juliana hadn't figured out how Miss Penny sensed her comings and goings, but she always did. Perhaps she was psychic or she had a motion detector trained on Juliana's assigned parking space.

Either way, true to form, Juliana had just stepped on her welcome mat when her neighbor cracked opened the front door directly across from her place. Miss Penny scanned Juliana from head to toes with her rheumy-eyed gaze. "Hello, Juliana. Late night at the campus job or were you coming from someplace else?"

Juliana turned politely and said, "Both. I came from somewhere else, and I was working on a special project for a writing job."

Miss Penny studied her face for a moment longer than usual, but it was as if she wasn't seeing Juliana at all.

"Everything okay, Miss Penny?"

The older woman dropped her intent gaze, shook a head with frizzled graying hair framing a wizened face and smiled. "I'm fine, just fine. And I think you'll be fine, too, young lady."

"Thanks, Miss Penny." Juliana didn't want to be rude, but she wanted to get inside. Miss Penny—as if sensing her hurry—had already closed her door.

Once inside her coveted first-floor apartment, she pulled the steno pad out of her purse, wondering again why she hadn't asked Diesel the "real" question she'd gone to get answered. All she'd managed were soft-ball queries regarding the cellular signal and far-out rumors about resident aliens.

She didn't remember writing the note to herself to check on cellular providers to discover if they had reason *not* to erect towers to deliver service in that area, but there it was on her notepad. Maybe there was a good reason. Or the renegade aliens had kept the towers out because it was easier to take over the world without immediate discovery. Juliana shook her head, closing her eyes in foolish defeat.

She'd been so fired up to find out about the Boogieman Affair? But had choked and never even brought the question up. What was wrong with her?

Had there truly been a malevolent creature loose in the streets of Alienn causing mayhem and chaos for the residents less than a year ago? Had it been swiftly covered up? Would she have the nerve to ask Diesel when he came over on Friday for lunch? She'd gone to ask him hard-hitting questions like an investigative reporter on the trail of a hot news story, and instead she'd kissed a gorgeous stranger like it was her job, on the flimsy premise that he *seemed* familiar, and promptly garnered a date for four days from now.

Juliana paused for a moment to relive that amazing kiss. She'd never kissed a veritable stranger before, but she'd been compelled to discover if Diesel tasted like she expected he would, which was totally crazy.

The kiss had been marvelous and exactly what she'd thought it would be. It had been perfect in every way, down to a resounding feeling of familiarity. And yet they'd never met before. Had they? No. She would have remembered him. No question in her mind on that score.

She pulled her purse off one shoulder and plopped it on the table by the front door. Keys still in her hand, she dropped them in the dish next to her purse. She was about to empty her pockets, but heard a strange noise outside her door. It sounded like someone had dropped something heavy on her porch, which then slid hard, bouncing against the bottom of the door.

Juliana peered through the peep hole, but saw nothing. She walked over to the left side of the door and peeked out the window. Nothing. She inhaled deeply and exhaled before opening the door a crack with the flimsy chain in place. She didn't see it at first, but then figured it out. She stared down and frowned. An apple with a single bite taken out of it rested against the threshold of her doorframe on her welcome mat. How rude and wasteful.

She picked it up, careful not to touch the eaten part, closed and re-locked her front door and threw the gnawed fruit in her kitchen trash next to the counter.

The sound of change in her pocket reminded her to return to the bowl where she kept her car keys and loose change and empty her pockets. There was nothing other than coins in one pocket, but in the other she was surprised to find a business card-sized piece of gray paper. Where had this come from?

One side featured the Big Bang Truck Stop logo and a coupon for five percent off a gas purchase.

She flipped the card over and read, "Maxwell the Martian says, Our Fearless Leader thinks you're very pretty, too."

What in the world was this?

Chapter Six

Diesel spent the next four days with nothing on his mind except Juliana and seeing her on Friday for lunch. He didn't make sense to most people. He often didn't answer questions with the correct answer. But he was also in a great mood, so everyone seemed to overlook his mistakes because his attitude was so improved.

He didn't mention his date with Juliana until the Thursday staff meeting late in the afternoon. It was a small group, which was good for dropping a bomb right before leaving.

Cam gave a report on security—reminding everyone to change their passwords again—as usual. Nova was taking notes, as usual. The first shot across the bow for discussions he didn't want to have was the announcement of the new gulag run he'd approved.

Axel finished the briefing on the UGG contract as a part of his general communications report. As expected, the elder council representative sat up after dozing through most of the meeting.

"Well, this is unexpected news! Why wasn't this subject brought up in the regular council meeting for approval last week?" Mr. Gris, the longest serving council rep, said and glared at Axel.

Axel's eyebrows went upward, and he sent Diesel a pitiful expression, looking for an official response. If he'd had the mental capabilities he would have shouted the word "coward" in Axel's direction. But he didn't and Axel probably already knew how he felt.

Before Mr. Gris could go on a long tirade, Diesel cleared his throat and quietly stood up. The elder moved his glare from Axel to Diesel. He told the elder in a quiet tone, "Because I didn't need approval. It was fully my decision to make. I planned to mention it at the regular council meeting next month as a courtesy."

Mr. Gris opened his mouth, closed it, fixed his stare on the center of the conference table and pressed his thin lips together, flattening them. He made a mild huffing noise and crossed his arms like an angry two-year-old about to launch into a full-blown tantrum.

"Anyone have anything else to discuss?" Diesel asked.

Everyone except the elder shook their heads and began gathering their things, getting ready to exit.

Nova stopped writing and started to stand, but Diesel said, "Wait a sec. I have one last thing to mention."

His subordinates looked at him. "I'm taking tomorrow off. If anyone needs anything, contact either Cam or Axel if you can't wait for my return." No one moved. No one said a thing.

Diesel said, "Okay. Good meeting. Until next Thursday, then."

"Hold up," Cam said. "Where are you going?"

"I just said I was taking the day off. What makes you think I'm going anywhere?"

Cam's eyes narrowed. "You just answered a question with a question and that is suspect."

Axel said, "Enjoy your time off."

Nova said, "You're meeting with that earthling again, aren't you?"

That roused Mr. Gris from his pout. "What earthling? Why doesn't anyone mention important stuff like a mysterious earthling? The council needs to be notified—"

Diesel blew a sharp whistle through his fingers, making even his own ears ring, and everyone stopped talking and moving at once.

"Listen up. I have been in charge for over a year. Before that I worked for a few years in preparation of taking over. I don't think taking one day off in all that time is asking so much. I'll say this one more time. I was offering the information as a courtesy. It's one day. I was not asking anyone's permission. Nor am I obliged to give anyone an itinerary. Meeting adjourned."

Diesel exited the room, knowing four shocked

gazes followed him out. He didn't care. He headed to his office in hopes of finding some peace and quiet.

Aunt Dixie was seated at Nova's desk. "You better not let Nova catch you there," he said in a low tone on his way by.

She stood up like a shot and followed him into his office as Nova entered the reception area.

"Were you sitting at my desk, Dixie Lou?" Nova asked.

"Course not. It's very uncomfortable anyway."

Nova rolled her eyes. Aunt Dixie stayed on his tail and closed his office door behind her. "Heard a rumor you're taking tomorrow off."

"That was fast." Somehow she'd gotten the information in the time it took him to exit the meeting room and get to his office, maybe twenty seconds. That might be a new record.

"Are you going to see someone, like a date?"

Diesel walked behind his desk and gave his aunt a sharp look. "How could you possibly know that?"

"I know things, Diesel." He shook his head. No one knew about this. He'd been tight-lipped all week on purpose.

"No doubt," he said under his breath as he sat in his chair. "Are you about to yell at me, too?"

"Course not. I'm all for it. You haven't had a day off in years."

"Thank you." Diesel looked up into her face. She

didn't look happy for him, exactly, but definitely very pleased with herself about something. She'd had the same look the day she came into the Cosmos Café with eight inches of her silver lamé uniform skirt whacked off and her hind end hanging out for all the world to see, insisting it was the only way she could earn a living wage.

"You're welcome. I hope you have fun."

Diesel wasn't fooled. She wasn't prone to wishing him well. More likely she was rubbing her hands together in glee and planning something diabolical in his short absence that he wouldn't approve of, but whatever, it would be someone else's problem tomorrow. He could deal with any Aunt Dixie fallout when he returned.

She turned to leave his office, but said over one shoulder, "Besides, it's about time you settled down and found a wife."

Now *that* was the Aunt Dixie he knew and loved. She was gone lickety-split, so he didn't bother responding, but he did smile for some unfathomable reason. Well, he fathomed it was because it made him happy thinking about pursuing Juliana as his future wife. However, it was way too early to hope for that.

This foray from his responsibilities was admittedly unusual, but he couldn't seem to help himself. He couldn't wait to see Juliana again.

Before the door closed all the way behind Aunt Dixie, Cam pushed it open and entered with a portable Defender in one hand. He plunked it down on the center of Diesel's desk.

"Take this with you, just in case."

"Just in case of what?" Diesel was *not* taking a Defender with him. He pushed it across the desk toward Cam. "I won't need it."

"I know where you're going." His brother pushed the white and blue Defender back to the center of the desk.

"Do you?"

"You're going to see that earthling. Take it." He gestured to the device. "You've been strange all week since meeting her. I saw the video of your second time speaking to her. You kissed her again."

"No, I didn't. She kissed me."

"Semantics." Cam leaned down and patted the Defender. "Take it."

"I'm not taking it, Cam. And if you press me, I'll change all my passwords to *p-a-s-s-w-o-r-d*."

Cam glared. "Fine. Go. Don't erase any of her memories. Do what you're going to do, but get her out of your system and move on. We don't need this kind of dangerous exposure."

"I hardly think a writer preparing a travelogue for a book comes to the level of dangerous exposure. Besides, I still maintain that our interstellar guest from Moogally wasn't authorized to use that emergency exit as an entrance back to the underground facility."

"I spoke to him. Turns out he drank too much

Gatorade and got disoriented. The exit was the only place he remembered he could get below."

"You mean he was drunk on his butt on a beverage known to alter his species' mental capabilities and he popped open an inappropriate door at the exact wrong time."

"Yes. That, too. Could have been worse. At least we contained the situation." He patted the Defender again as if it had been the perfect solution. It hadn't. Diesel had lost time with Juliana. Important time. Time he dearly wished he could get back.

"She's never going to remember the first time we met. For me, that is worse."

Cam leaned over and planted his palms flat on Diesel's desk. "She's also never going to remember that she saw a non-humanoid alien at the Big Bang Truck Stop in Alienn, Arkansas. She's never going to write about that incident in her article or travel book or whatever. That's the more important fact, Diesel. *That's* what you should be thinking about."

"Is it?"

"What is up with you?"

Diesel pushed out a sigh. "I really like her."

"I'm aware. But you should get used to the idea that you absolutely cannot keep her."

"She's not some stray pet I took in, Cam."

"She's an earthling and not meant for you, Diesel."

"There isn't a law against—"

"Well, there should be."

"Why?"

A distant look came over his brother's face. Diesel had never seen Cam display emotion like this before. "Maybe I don't want you to get hurt."

"Did *you* get hurt?"

Cam was very private about everything, but until a couple of years ago, he'd been much less uptight about absolutely everything. At the time, Diesel had thought Cam was merely stepping up to make a name for himself in his new position as Security Officer. Perhaps his brother had been burned by love and buried himself in his work.

"No comment." Cam scooped the Defender up, executed a perfect about-face and exited the office without another word. Diesel would have to inquire about Cam's issues later; it was time to get ready for his trip tomorrow.

The intercom on his desk buzzed. Nova's voice came through the small speaker. "There's a call for you on line one."

"Thank you."

"It's Juliana Masters," she said in an amused tone of voice, like she was tattling on someone.

Diesel locked his eyes on a festively colored piece of paper on his desk to keep from rolling them. "Thank you." He clicked off and pushed the line one button, hoping Juliana wasn't about to call off their meeting after so much drama had been attached to his merely taking a day off.

"Hello." He tried to sound nonchalant, as if he didn't care one iota if she canceled last minute.

"Hi, Diesel. It's Juliana. I wanted to make sure we were still on for tomorrow."

"Yes. I'll be there at eleven as you requested."

"Great. I'll see you then." She hung up quickly. Was she having second thoughts? Was he about to be disappointed in their meeting tomorrow?

Diesel inhaled deeply and exhaled as much stress out of his body as he could. He didn't know what to expect, but decided to be prepared for anything and do his best not to get too attached.

Cam was right about one thing—if Diesel got too involved with Juliana, he'd have to be very careful. The largest reason earthlings and Alphas were discouraged from marrying was because the ruling party did not want any indigenous people to have knowledge of their operation. He hadn't heard it lately, but the phrase *loose lips, sink ships* had been used in relation to any earthlings discovering they were here.

The few Alpha-human relationships he'd ever heard of had been allowed because the couple in question went back to Alpha-Prime. Diesel wanted to live on Earth. He wanted to be near his family.

Alpha-Prime was a good place to live, but he'd spent the bulk of his life on Earth. It was more his home than the planet his family had come from. His parents had come as newlyweds with dreams of making Earth their permanent residence. Diesel had been born on Earth, making him technically an earthling, except that he was one hundred percent Alpha-Prime alien.

Diesel liked Juliana, but if they had a chance to be together, he'd have to keep her in the dark about where his parents had immigrated from, which was an entire galaxy away from Earth. Hard to do with a spouse, especially if he expected to stay the Fearless Leader of this operation, and he did want to keep his job.

The secrecy that would be required for a lifetime was daunting. That was really why no Alpha had ever married a human. Would he be the first? Would he simply ditch his family and his responsibilities here to move back to Alpha-Prime with his human wife?

Or would he cave like almost everyone else had, and distance himself from someone he loved? Or, worse, spend a lifetime either drugging her into forgetting things she should know or blasting her in the face with the Defender to keep her knowledge of his alien identity and his parents' planet of origin completely erased.

Chapter Seven

Friday morning, Doraydo, Arkansas

Juliana fretted over every single detail while getting ready for Diesel to show up. She wanted to ask him a bunch of questions—the ones she'd neglected to ask the first time they met, especially the one regarding the dark entity she'd heard was caught roaming around causing trouble in the Boogieman Affair.

She also wanted to kiss his hiking boots off and discover if he was looking for a girlfriend. If not, perhaps she could ask him for a job. No. That would be weird. The job would keep her here in southern Arkansas. Did she want that? Not up until she'd met Diesel. In fact, she had relished the idea of the money she'd earn with the article because she wanted to travel back to Washington State and investigate her own past.

In the meantime, was she looking for a boyfriend? *Maybe*. Someone to share her lonely life with? *Getting warmer.* A husband? *Ding-Ding-Ding.* Definitely.

She did want to get married, of course, and she especially wanted a huge family with a greater than average number of children, but until meeting Diesel a few days ago, she had expected to be alone for the remainder of her life.

Since that disastrous, child-hating boyfriend in her first year of college, she'd only dated sporadically, usually because of well-meaning friends' blind date setups and never more than once with any guy. Was that pathetic? Maybe.

Miss Penny told her once there were worse things than living alone. Juliana wasn't certain that was true.

While she expected to spend her life alone, it wasn't what she longed for. Each year that went by without any prospects made her more and more sad about her future.

Juliana wanted a big family. She wanted holidays filled with lots of laughter, lots of family and lots of memories. She had no memories of her parents or any family members. That was why she was so determined to find answers.

She loved being among books as part of her regular job in the campus library, but eventually she'd have to get a job that paid more.

If she wrote a great article for Finder's—whether she found evidence of aliens roaming in Alienn, Arkansas or not—the bonus money would give her enough to travel for a while and ultimately move forward with her life.

But for the first time since she started college, she wanted to remain in the area and explore the boyfriend potential she saw in the Fearless Leader of a famous local truck stop.

Meeting Diesel had somehow changed the anxious feeling in her bones that she needed to leave the area as soon as possible. That deep, annoying, uneasy feeling had been part of her life since leaving the orphanage. Something about Diesel made it dissipate. He made her feel safe and she wanted to feel safe. He also generated some rather salacious thoughts, especially at night, starring Diesel completely naked and in her bed. She'd never felt that with any other man. Ever.

She glanced at the clock. Only an hour until he arrived. She'd gotten up at the crack of dawn to prepare. Everything was in place. Juliana had even cooked, preparing homemade soup. She wanted to impress him. She wanted him to like her. She wanted him to kiss her again. She wanted to lure him to her bedroom. Should she try it? Would he go?

There was a sound at her front door. Was he early? Was he as anxious as she was to meet up again?

Juliana walked toward her entryway and heard something knock against the outside of the door.

She popped it open without checking through the peephole, expecting to see Diesel, but no one stood there. She looked down and saw another apple with a single bite taken out of it dead center on her welcome mat. Again? Really?

Juliana looked to the left out into the parking area. Nothing. To the right was a central garden area between the apartment buildings. No one was around.

Miss Penny opened her door. "Hello, Juliana."

"Hi, Miss Penny." She picked up the apple to carry it inside.

"What are you doing today?" her neighbor asked pleasantly.

"Actually, I have a date in a little while."

Miss Penny's weathered face melted into a fierce frown. Juliana paused, struck by surprise. She'd never seen Miss Penny frown before. Just as quickly as she'd shown unhappiness, Miss Penny softened, losing her stern expression. Even so, she didn't quite smile when she asked, "You have a date? Land sakes, child, that sounds exciting."

"I hope so." Juliana grinned, unable to help herself.

Miss Penny tilted her head to one side. "So who is this young man?"

"His name is Diesel Grey. He's the...uh...manager at a truck stop."

For a moment, Miss Penny looked as if she'd

decided Juliana was only joking, but then realized Diesel wasn't some figment of her imagination and was actually a living, breathing human coming to call.

Her wrinkled brows furrowed. "How on earth did you meet him?"

"Oh, I'm working on a special project for Finder's. I went to ask him some question about Alienn, Arkansas."

Miss Penny's eyes widened. "Very interesting."

"I hope so." Juliana didn't want to be rude, but she had a few more chores to complete before Diesel arrived. "I'll let you know how things go."

"I'll look forward to that. I want to hear everything."

Juliana walked back into her apartment, chucked the apple in the trash container and went to change. A thrill rode down her spine as she looked forward to her coming date. First, they'd chat. Then they'd eat. Then she'd ask him a few innocuous questions. Then she'd hit him with the hard questions and see if he tried to kiss her senseless again to avoid answering them.

Either he'd give her some insight into the rumors or she'd get to kiss him. Both choices counted as a win as far as she was concerned. She'd never been so eager to get a man into her bed before. Was Diesel the one?

Ten minutes before he was due, her doorbell

sounded. She fairly skipped over to the entrance, opening the door without looking out the peephole.

There he stood in all his gorgeousness. In one hand he held a small bouquet of flowers rich with the colors pink and white. In the other he held a very large slice of red velvet cake in a clear plastic container. It was known in some circles as the state dessert of Arkansas. Juliana couldn't believe he'd brought anything at all.

"Hello," she said exuberantly, her eyes feasting on the gifts he'd brought. "Please come in."

He stepped across her threshold and Juliana closed the door before Miss Penny could get a look at him. She heard her neighbor's door crack open just as her front door clicked shut. Miss Penny could grill her later.

Diesel handed her the flowers and the clear container. "I hope you like red velvet cake."

"I love it. Every self-respecting Southerner does." Technically, she was a transplanted Southerner, but she wanted to be one and who would test her?

"Probably true." He grinned. "It smells good in here. What's for lunch?"

"Soup. I made it myself. Hope you like it."

"I'm certain I—" He stopped talking in mid-sentence as he looked down into her kitchen wastebasket.

"What's wrong?"

His severe cobalt gaze came up to sear her with intensity. "The apple."

She placed the flowers and dessert on the counter. "I found it on my doorstep. I didn't waste it, if that's what you're worried about."

He looked horrified for a second. "On your doorstep. When did *this* happen?"

"About an hour ago. Why?"

Diesel spun around and marched to the door. Popping it open, he leaned out to survey the outside as though he expected to see any number of bad guys swarming the area.

"What's going on?" Juliana approached. "What's wrong?"

He stepped inside, closed the door and locked it.

"You're scaring me," she said when he secured the chain up top.

Diesel turned and put his hands on her shoulders. "I'm sorry. I don't mean to frighten you."

"What's the big deal about a half-eaten apple on my doorstep?"

He got that expression on his face, the one that made her think he might kiss her to keep from answering her questions.

Luckily, she was right.

Diesel squeezed her shoulders and planted his amazing lips on hers without saying a word. In response, Juliana launched herself at him, wrapping her arms around his neck and clinging to him until he slid his arms around her back and lifted her to her tip-toes, all the while kissing her socks off.

Diesel kissed Juliana as if his life depended on it. As if this would be the last time he was able to before some unknown entity smoked them where they stood. Kissing. Gloriously kissing. His mind also glancing into a forbidden arena he shouldn't dare contemplate. Not yet. Maybe not ever.

However, in his world, an apple with a single bite from it tossed on the doorstep of someone's home was a veiled threat. It meant, *watch out. Don't continue with your current path. If you keep asking about this, or doing this—whatever it was—your life may be in jeopardy.*

It was more commonly used as a deterrent in romance. *Stay away from my love interest.* But he didn't have a love interest. Juliana was his only love interest. No one even knew about her, at least not yet.

He worried about her safety if they continued. Who could possibly know about them? As he ticked off names in his head, the number was bigger than just a few. There was Cam, Nova, Aunt Dixie, Paulo the truck stop clerk, Axel, the elder, Mr. Gris and, of course, anyone *they'd* told. His rather rash exit after yesterday's weekly truck stop staff meeting might have notified a few more. The grapevine at Big Bang was healthy and well.

Space potatoes. A whole legion of folks could already know about this relationship.

His first thought was Cam, who'd been rather vocal in his disapproval of Diesel dating a human. No. Cam wouldn't do this. Would he? Diesel didn't want to believe it. Even so, he planned to grill his brother later.

In the meantime, Juliana tasted as good as she had several days ago. Diesel was definitely smitten with this very beautiful human. Cam had told him to get her out of his system. Diesel didn't think he'd ever get her out of his system. Nor did he want to try. Cam could suck it.

Once they stopped kissing, if they ever did, he'd have to explain his actions and worry about the apple in her wastebasket. He'd gone too far. He should have internalized his fears at first and quietly discovered where it had come from. For all he knew there was a wasteful, spoiled child out there who'd tossed the apple after one bite because it wasn't pizza or junk food.

But in this moment he soaked up the intimate time with Juliana, rubbing his lips over hers again and again, relishing the connection.

She broke away, resting her forehead on his, breathing hard. Soon she whispered, "I thought about kissing you all week."

"So did I," he whispered back.

"I missed you. Is that strange?" Her soft fingertips brushed along his jaw, sending his thoughts to a more wild and wicked place once more.

Yeah, I'm never getting you out of my system.

"No. Or at least I hope not, because then I'm just as strange."

"Good. I think." She laughed and eased away from him, yet still resting in his loose embrace. Her expression sobered. "Why were you so upset about the apple?"

Diesel contemplated any number of lies he could tell and get her to believe, but couldn't bring himself to do it. "Where I come from, it's considered a mild threat, especially where romance is concerned."

"Really? I've never heard of that before. Is that exclusive to southern Arkansas only or elsewhere, too?"

He shrugged. "Not sure exactly. Might just be a family thing. I'm sorry if I scared you. I was just surprised." *Boy howdy, what a shocker!* "It's not like a mafia hitman threat where your life is in danger or anything. More in the realm of old wives' tales and the like." *Sort of.*

"Do you have a jealous girlfriend tucked away somewhere?"

"Nah. I'm single." *Not counting the unlikely but feasibly possible arranged marriage to someone on another planet—someone I've never met. Otherwise, no.*

"Good. I'm single, too."

Diesel leaned down and kissed her again. He brushed his hands down her back, pulling her closer against his body...for about four seconds until a buzzer went off in the kitchen.

"My soup," Juliana said, tearing herself away from him to go to the small kitchen and tend to a steaming pot on her stove. She put a big wooden spoon into the steamy and heavenly scented concoction. She scooped a portion of soup into the oversized spoon, pursed her lips to blow on it and turned to him, offering a taste.

"It's bacon, sausage and potato with vegetables."

"You had me at bacon," he said with a smile, leaning in to get a slurped taste of bacon-flavored goodness.

He moaned in appreciation. "That's really good."

"I'm glad. I'll ladle us some into bowls. Have a seat at the table and I'll bring it to you."

"Thanks." The table was already set so he seated himself and let her do her thing. She brought two large bowls of the soup and then pulled a sheet pan out of the oven filled with what looked like homemade biscuits.

The soup was delicious and the biscuits were divine. When they'd finished with lunch, she put the slice of red velvet cake he'd brought on a small plate along with two forks so they could share it.

Between the first two bites of cake, Diesel asked, "So, what is your article about again? Is it on

Alienn exclusively or just in general seeking any and all information on bloodthirsty aliens trying to take over Earth?"

"Very funny." Her smile could light up his soul. "My article has to do with either proving or disproving the existence of aliens hiding in plain sight. My former teacher—the one who recommended me for this project—wants me to prove it. He thinks the article will help sell more books if there is a juicy suggestion regarding aliens roaming around nearby.

"The possibility that readers could come here using a Finder's book to see it for themselves would also be a boon. Although I can't imagine I'm the only one he's ever tried to wrangle into writing it."

They finished the cake, Diesel offering her the final bite. Juliana took it and then scooped up a fallen glob of frosting with her finger, cleaning the plate completely.

She gathered the dishes and Diesel helped her carry them to the sink. Once she'd loaded her small dishwasher, they started walking toward the living room.

"What's his name? Your old teacher, I mean," Diesel asked.

"Mr. Harriman."

Diesel searched his memory. He'd never heard of him. "Did he provide all the rumors regarding Alienn?"

"Perhaps." Juliana looked a bit uncomfortable.

"There is actually one other thing I meant to ask before I left last week, but I decided to wait until we were alone."

"Okay." Diesel straightened. *Here it comes.* He quickly rehearsed the company line about the Boogieman Affair in his head.

"Do you ever want to have children?"

His mouth opened but no words came out. Juliana certainly had the ability to take him off guard at every turn.

"Children?"

"Yes, you know—small human beings. They're very tiny and cute."

His brows furrowed. Hadn't they already discussed this before? No. Wait. That had been a part of the conversation before her memory got wiped by the Big D.

Dang Cam's security-minded hide.

Diesel closed his eyes and then opened them again. He fixed a stare directly into her baby blues and said, "Yes, Juliana. I do want children someday. I come from a pretty large family."

"Oh? How large?"

"There are seven of us."

"Seven? Really? Awesome." Her elated expression mirrored the one she'd displayed the first time he'd answered the question.

"How about you?" He'd neglected to ask last time, thanks to octo-man ruining the mood. "Do you have a big family?"

Her expression immediately shuttered. "Um…no. I don't have any at all."

"None?" His cousin Stella Grey was an only child. Her parents had died tragically on their home planet, leaving her technically an orphan, but at least Stella had been transferred to Earth to stay with his family.

"Nope. I was left on the doorstep of a church when I was a baby."

"In Arkansas?"

"Washington State. A very small place called Gray's Harbor City."

"Gray's Harbor? I wonder if I have kin up there," Diesel said, knowing full well he didn't.

"It's spelled different, but you never know."

"How did you end up going to school in Arkansas?"

"I got a grant to go to college in Missouri. After I graduated, I earned another grant for graduate school here in Doraydo, provided I studied communications. So I did. I graduated in the spring with honors."

"Was it alien communications you studied?" he asked with a grin.

"Perhaps. So, are you ready to talk about the Boogieman Affair, yet?"

Chapter 8

"What?" Diesel looked shell-shocked. Juliana didn't want to talk about her lonely, pathetic existence on this planet anymore, so she pivoted.

"That's the other question I forgot to ask you last time we were together. The truth is, I didn't really forget. I just wanted to ask it when we were alone."

Diesel didn't answer. Instead, he stepped closer and kissed her again very thoroughly, very firmly, very aggressively. It was amazing. Juliana enjoyed it for a few minutes and then pulled her mouth from his. "You can't keep kissing me every time I ask a question you don't want to answer."

"Why not? I like kissing you." He slid his palms along her face gently, dropped them to her shoulders and then to her back, pulled her close, stared into her eyes and kissed her again. Passionately, like it had been done since the dawn of humanity when a man wanted to coax a woman into a deeper…connection.

She was lost to it. Lost to him. Wanted him. Needed him.

Juliana danced him backward toward her bedroom. He was the first man she'd ever wanted to take there…needed to take there.

She couldn't wait another second to discover what it felt like to be pressed to him, naked. She'd thought about this rather scandalous prospect all week, hoping he didn't change his mind or cancel their date.

Crap.

This was their first date. She shouldn't sleep with him on their first date. What would it say about her if she lured him to her bedroom in the first hour they were together? She slowed her pace, clinching him tighter, kissing him harder.

Then she thought of something. He'd told her he didn't shapeshift on the first date. But when? Juliana remembered it like a dream. Like the dream she'd had before waking up in her car and meeting him in the convenience store. Wait. How could that be? That *had* been a dream hadn't it?

Juliana remembered another very important something. She stopped moving toward her bedroom. She should straighten this one important thing out first.

He stopped, opened his eyes and noticed they'd drifted halfway down the hallway to her bedroom.

His gaze moved to her open bedroom door. The corner of her bed was visible from where they stood.

"I need to show you something," she said quietly, knowing if she didn't stop them now, they'd be on that bed, if she had her way.

"Okay," he said, and cleared his throat.

She released him and returned to her living room. He cleared his throat again, straightened to his full height and moved to follow her. She bent and pulled the small gray card from a box on the coffee table.

"It's not another apple is it?" he asked, the sound of his concern growing again.

"No." Juliana handed Diesel the card. "What do you make of this?" She studied him closely for his reaction.

He held the card up and frowned. He looked at it, flipped it over and then his eyes grew as big as plates. The wide-eyed gaze shifted in her direction.

"Where did you get this?"

"I found that in my pocket when I got home from meeting you at the truck stop. But the funny thing is that I dreamed about it before ever meeting you."

"You had a dream about this?" he asked in a stern tone. "What dream?"

She nodded at the card. "The one where you pushed my hand against the Maxwell the Martian fortune-teller box and this was the fortune that came out. It seemed so real I wanted to ask if you remembered it."

Diesel forced a smile and a puzzled squint. "How could I remember your dream?" *How could you be dreaming about something the Defender erased from your mind?*

"Maybe I didn't dream it. Maybe you used your mind control on me and I forgot," she said with a laugh. Her gaze was steady, inquiring, emboldened as if she wanted to ensure he hadn't truly used his non-existent powers of mind control.

He couldn't muster even a glimmer of a smile. He didn't respond to her shocking knowledge. "Care if I keep this?" he asked.

She snatched it from his fingers. "I'd rather keep it, if you don't mind."

Diesel's head was swimming with questions and worries and not all of them coming from her. He still had to address the threatening apple issue, vowing to discuss it with Cam. But right now he should go back to Alienn and talk to his security-minded brother about the Big D and its apparent failure.

It was a task he suddenly wanted to avoid, because he worried what Cam might do to Juliana if the Defender didn't work to erase her memories. He'd probably want to use the old method of human memory erasure, the one that involved big syringes. Diesel decided he didn't want to share this information with anyone. He'd have to research her possible dream memories on his own.

"I should go," Diesel said absently. *I need to either figure this out quickly or, worst-case scenario, talk to Cam. Pronto.*

"You're leaving?" Her question came out sounding so forlorn he reconsidered his options.

Diesel checked his watch. It was not very late. He'd only been here an hour. He should go. But he really wanted to stay.

If he hadn't been mistaken, right before this disturbing dream revelation, she'd been leading him toward her bedroom. While he wanted to go in there and explore Juliana more than anything in this world, he also needed to consider all the interesting facts zipping through his head. Like the disturbing memories she shouldn't have. Like the fortune card he should have collected.

His earlier conversation with Cam slid into his mind. What if he'd taken the portable Defender Cam had offered? Would Diesel really have been able to snatch the card from her fingers, whip out the weapon and zap her for only five minutes to keep her from remembering it? Ugh. He sounded like Cam. Did he want to zap her again? No, never again.

Besides, if she was having dreams about that supposedly erased time, he had larger issues. It would be so much easier to tell her the truth, the whole truth and nothing but the truth. He'd do it if he wasn't convinced Cam would throttle him and drop a still-experimental Defender bomb on Juliana's head once he was incapacitated.

Diesel studied her beautiful eyes and calmed down. She put a hand on his arm and he relaxed even more. "Don't go yet," she said. "I didn't mean to make you angry."

"I'm not angry." *Not at you.* He pointed to the card in her hand. "I don't get it. I don't know where it came from. Is it possible you picked it up in the truck stop somewhere and simply forgot about it?"

She pondered what he'd said, looking down at the card. She appeared uncertain. "I guess it's possible." She frowned, but put the card back in the box on her coffee table.

"What else would you like to talk about?" Diesel asked.

She bit her lip.

"It's okay, Juliana. Ask me whatever you want to know."

"Will you answer the question I asked about the Boogieman Affair?"

Diesel took a deep breath. "Sure. That was just blown out of proportion. It was a story about a stray, injured dog that had the element of a childish telephone game added to it."

"What does that mean?" Her beautiful brow furrowed.

Diesel moved closer, wanting to fold her into his embrace. "It started out as a report of an injured dog on the outskirts of town. When our animal control people went to look, they couldn't find him right away. By the time that evening ended, there were outlandish reports of an entity skulking around town inflicting evil on everyone it saw, which was not accurate."

"Really?"

"Yep."

"That's the company line?"

He lifted one shoulder and let it drop. "That's the story as I know it."

"So it's not like the monster from the Legend of Boggy Creek in Fouke, Arkansas or anything like that?"

He shook his head. "That story was way before my time, but no, nothing like that in this case."

"I see." She thought over what he'd said for a few seconds and a winsome smile appeared on her face. "Are you going to forever kiss me whenever you don't want to talk about something?"

"Probably," he said, taking a step closer, wanting to resume their earlier steamy kiss. "It's obviously more fun than erasing your thoughts, puny earthling."

Juliana seemed to relax. Diesel drew her into his arms again. The kiss they shared was as gentle as he could make it. He could stay in this moment for a lifetime and be content. Kissing Juliana was exquisite. *She* was exquisite. The dance began again as they kissed and embraced and kissed. Juliana wrapped her arms around his middle, pulling him backward toward her hallway and presumably her bedroom once again.

He shouldn't go. He shouldn't allow her to lead him there. Diesel wanted to go to her room more than he'd ever wanted anything in his life. What might happen there? Diesel couldn't wait to find out.

Ding-dong. Ding-dong. Ding-dong.

The doorbell startled them out of their sensual journey. The first ding broke them apart. The rest weren't needed, as the sound had the effect of pouring icy cold water on any further kissing or dancing down the hall toward her bedroom.

Juliana pushed out a frustrated-sounding sigh. She dropped her arms from him and moved toward the door, grumbling under her breath words he couldn't hear, but that made him smile nonetheless.

The thought of the apple in the trash made him move quickly to step in front of the door and keep her from opening it. He should take that apple back to the labs downstairs at the truck stop just to see if anyone had been foolish enough to leave behind DNA.

"Wait," he said, peeking out the peephole to discover the ding-donger's identity. He saw graying hair. He mentally reached out through the door, hoping to ascertain the thoughts of the person outside and any possible threat they might pose, but got nothing.

He stood beside Juliana as she opened the door.

"Miss Penny?" Juliana sounded shocked. Diesel eyed the wizened old woman on her doorstep suspiciously. "What are you doing here?"

Miss Penny gave Diesel a long, hard look from head to boots. "I wanted to see what the young man who'd caught your eye looked like, that's all," she said with a wan, tired smile. "Aren't you going to invite me in?"

"Sure." Juliana stood aside. The older woman crossed the threshold slowly, taking small steps and seeming to look even more tired than when she stood outside.

Once Juliana had closed her front door, Diesel extended his hand to Miss Penny. "Hi. I'm Diesel Grey."

She had a surprisingly firm grip. "Hi yourself. You can call me Miss Penny." She nodded once at Juliana. "She and I look after each other."

"Good for you." Diesel tried to read the older woman's thoughts again. He got the sense she didn't mean any harm or have any disconcerting agenda toward either of them. Miss Penny was even more difficult to read than the woman he was falling in love with. Maybe Diesel was losing what little mind-reading skill he had as he aged. A depressing thought he tucked away for a much later time.

He cleared his throat as the *falling in love with*

notion soaked back into his brain. He promptly looked in Juliana's direction as if he'd see that sentiment written in a cartoon bubble over their heads, giving away his latest secret.

"He's handsome, I'll give you that," Miss Penny murmured to Juliana, as he contemplated what future—if any—they could have together. Was a life together possible on Earth? Maybe. If Diesel could have his way, he wanted the rest of his life to be entwined with Juliana's. She was special and he was smart enough to know it.

"Thank you," Diesel said. "Where are you from, Miss Penny?"

"Oh, here and there. Been lots of places in my long life, that's for sure," she said with a wink. "I understand you're the manager of a truck stop. Is that true?" Her tone had shifted to one sounding more like a father asking a suitor about his intentions rather than a neighbor casually asking after his career goals.

"Yes. I run the Big Bang Truck Stop in Alienn, Arkansas. Have you heard of it?"

She nodded. "Lots of rumors associated with Alienn. Little green men and the like running around causing all kinds of trouble and chaos. But I guess you already know all about that."

Diesel chuckled good-naturedly. "I do. It's hard not to get attention when we put up so many billboards with cartoon aliens along Route 88 to bring folks into the truck stop."

"Oh, now, I *like* those billboards. Very clever. Very funny."

"Thank you," Diesel said for a second time.

"Is that how you and Juliana met? Is she investigating you?"

"As a matter of fact, yes, that's exactly how we met."

"Is she going to get you to reveal any secrets with her feminine wiles?" Her gaze traveled from the two of them to the hallway they'd just been moseying down toward Juliana's bedroom. The implication was clear.

"Miss Penny!" Juliana said. "Feminine wiles, really? What is up with you?" She blushed profusely and Diesel fell a little bit more in love with her. Hard not to.

"I guess *that* struck a nerve," Miss Penny said. "I suppose my work here is done then." She turned to leave. "Are you still going to be able to take me grocery shopping this afternoon?"

"Was that today?" Juliana asked. An expression of guilt crossed her features. "I'm sorry. I must have forgotten."

"That's okay, dear. I know you've had a lot on your mind lately." She gave Diesel a onceover from head to boots again. "I'll just get a taxi or something."

"No!" Juliana exclaimed. "I'll take you. When do you want to go?"

"Half an hour? Will that be enough…I mean,

will that be okay?" Diesel read between the lines of her short question. What she really meant to say was, "Is that time enough for the two of you to say goodbye but not enough time to mosey down to the bedroom?"

"Sure."

"Thank you, dear. I'll come back and knock on your door after I fetch my list." Miss Penny hurried to the entrance, popped it open and was crossing the threshold at a clip faster than Diesel could have imagined her moving that shriveled, frail-looking little body of hers. The door closed with a hearty thump, belying the woman's fragile strength.

Juliana looked disappointed. She glanced very briefly at her hallway and back into his face. "I'm sorry. I forgot I'd promised to take her to the grocery store. I should have picked a different day."

"No problem. I should get back anyway." Diesel forced himself not to look longingly in the direction of her bedroom. It didn't really matter. It was too soon. He knew it was. He would have stopped any sexual entanglement, wouldn't he? Probably. Maybe.

Unless she'd insisted. *How can I resist her?*

Juliana put a hand on his shoulder, distracting his wayward thoughts. "When will I see you again?"

Diesel grabbed her hand, putting it between his palms. "I don't know," he replied with a grin, "but I can't wait."

He glanced at her trash can and asked if he could take the menacing apple with him. She picked it up. Careful not to touch the eaten part, she dropped it into a plastic sandwich bag and handed it to him.

"Thanks. I have a friend in local law enforcement." *He's my brother who works in the basement.* "I'll find out if he can analyze it for me. Probably nothing will come of it, but you never know."

She nodded and a smile shaped her lovely mouth. "Maybe I could come back to Alienn next time. I still need to get some details for my article." *Was that a good idea?* Diesel wasn't certain, but he also wanted to see her again as soon as possible.

"Are you busy tomorrow night?" he asked, thinking about the typical way he spent Saturday evenings, which was either at work catching up on boring bookkeeping, or at home utterly alone.

"Saturday night? I figured that would be a busy night for you."

"Any night can be busy, depending on the various trucking schedules. Doesn't mean I need to be there every single moment, right?" *Unless you talk to certain members of my family. Some folks think I should live there right in my office.*

"Okay. Where should I meet you?"

"How about my office at the truck stop? And then if you'd like, I'll give you a mini tour of the town. You can get actual facts for your article instead of innuendos and speculation about scary monsters running wild in town. What do you think?"

"Excellent. I would love that."

"Good. I'll look forward to it. I'll even make you dinner."

"You cook?"

He shrugged, uncomfortable in the role of bachelor chef. "I've been known to grill a burger or two. Besides, you cooked for me. Seems only fair to return the favor."

"Thank you. And I appreciate your willingness to help me with my article. It means a lot to me. Maybe you could tell me a few stories or interesting historical things about the town of Alienn to write about instead of aliens hiding in plain sight."

"My pleasure." Diesel could tell her lots of alien-related stories, and how he personally lived his alien life in plain sight, but he took the out she offered, figuring he'd stick to a couple of old facts and tidbits few outsiders would know about Alienn.

"I also want you to know that my intent isn't to cause any trouble for you or your town. I'm just trying to write an interesting article for a travel book."

He nodded. "Good."

"The rumors about Alienn aren't new, obviously, but what I heard about the Boogieman Affair is certainly tantalizing. If it was only a wounded dog loose in town and the incident was overly dramatized, I'll certainly make that my ultimate conclusion for the piece. But I'd love to have information or a story no one else has or that few people know about."

"I'll scout around and see if I can come up with something interesting for your article."

"Thank you, Diesel. Also, I'd be willing to give you an advance copy to read."

"I'd appreciate that." He glanced at his watch. "I'd better get out of here so you can take Miss Penny shopping."

Juliana already had her hand on his forearm. She squeezed briefly, getting his attention. "Sorry we were interrupted."

"Don't worry about it." Diesel did kiss her again though. It was a lingering kiss, filled with as much restrained passion as he could muster. He broke their embrace before he wanted to, but was grateful he'd see her tomorrow. He'd have time to consider all the issues he faced contemplating a life with an engaging earthling and whether he'd have to give up his job at the truck stop and move to another galaxy with her.

"I'll see you tomorrow night," she said with a sweet smile.

"Can't wait." He moved toward her front door, not wanting to leave her, knowing he needed to go and think about things, not the least of which was preparing his family for her visit.

They would want full disclosure as to his intentions regarding Juliana as someone important in his life—especially Cam—and then he'd take her to his place in Alienn. He wanted her to see his home. Also, he wanted her.

Before he could stop himself, Diesel pulled her close, kissed her hard, passionately and quickly, and left before they had the opportunity to start dancing back toward her bedroom.

If he stayed a moment longer, kissing her in that way any longer, that's exactly where they'd end up.

Chapter 9

Juliana had driven the familiar distance from Doraydo to Alienn in record time. She parked in the same spot as last time, turning the car off purposefully since she didn't have the memory of doing it last time.

During her previous visit, she'd woken up slumped in the front seat of her car like a two-year-old who missed a nap.

Not wanting to make the same mistake, she took a late afternoon nap before driving to Alienn to ensure she was awake for tonight's "date" or whatever it was.

She'd even packed an overnight bag and socked it away in her trunk, just in case she ended up unable to drive herself home. Not that they'd end up in bed together, necessarily, but what if they split a bottle of wine, or two?

Or what if they had several cocktails during

whatever dinner he prepared? What if she drank too much? She would never drive after drinking, so the overnight bag was not presumptuous at all, right? It was for safety's sake. She told herself the lie over and over to feel better about the fact she was presuming quite a lot.

Juliana got out of her car, locked it, slung her purse over one shoulder and entered the Big Bang Truck Stop convenience store.

Instead of Paulo, the clerk she spoke to last time, a young woman also dressed in silver lamé watched Juliana from behind the low cashier's counter. Her sparkly shirt showed quite a bit more cleavage than Paulo's. She was seated on a stool, heels dug into the spindles below to keep her balance. Her arms were crossed as if ready to do battle, which also helped showcase her more than ample boobs to a greater extent. She was very pretty and slender, with shoulder-length dark hair and striking blue eyes that seemed to spark with electricity.

She likely would have been prettier if she smiled. So far, she hadn't. She wasn't wearing a nametag, but Juliana smiled and approached the counter to ask directions to Diesel's office and ensure she knew where she was going.

The woman didn't smile in return. Instead, she seemed to study Juliana with a judgy gaze. Given her expression, she obviously found Juliana wanting.

"Help you," she said, not asking, but demanding in a curt, impolite tone. Juliana wasn't the sort of person who would rat out an employee for being discourteous, but this woman—someone she'd never seen before today—made her reconsider.

Juliana dropped her smile and said, "I'm looking for Diesel Grey's office. It's in the back corner, right?"

The woman's mouth pursed until it looked like she'd just sucked the core out of a vinegar-soaked lemon. She took quite a long time to come up with a single-word response. "Right." Her gaze intensified with growing hostility.

Juliana looked back at her for only a moment, wondering what her problem was. As she walked away, another woman came into the store, voicing a loud complaint about the water in the window washer containers not being clean enough. "How often do you change them? Once a year whether they need it or not?" the wound-up woman accused.

Juliana expected the woman behind the counter to growl the customer out of the store, but instead she heard, "Oh no. I'm so sorry, ma'am," in a tone that sounded as sweet as honey-soaked cake. "That's just completely inexcusable on our part. I'll send someone outside right away to change it for you."

Juliana looked over her shoulder to see the clerk

pick up an old-style phone, push a couple of digits and ask in another very syrupy tone for someone to service the wiper stations out by the pumps.

The customer was also surprised by the swift positive response, stammering, "Well...um...thanks for getting right on this." She left the store, presumably to head back to her car.

Juliana narrowed her eyes at the girl behind the counter. She returned back to her arms crossed, attitude-filled stare when she noticed Juliana watching her. Curious.

She didn't know what she'd done to earn the wrath of this woman, but brushed it off and headed for the Fearless Leader's office.

Juliana noticed a fortune-teller box with Maxwell the Martian inside. She stopped in front of the small, telephone booth-sized prop as a powerful memory slid into her brain. *Diesel stood behind her with his palm pressing firmly against her hand. Together pushing in and holding the red button down to receive the fortune as his whole amazing body connected with her from shoulder blades to thighs.*

She touched the button again, holding it down as she remembered how good Diesel smelled, standing so close to her, when he'd helped her get a fortune from the machine. The last kiss they shared suddenly lit her imagination up with possibilities for tonight's meeting. What would happen? She couldn't wait to find out.

Maxwell started moving in a jerky fashion. The

small alien's lips started moving in an erratic, mechanical way. "Bing Boing Boppity Bop Boing Bing Bing!" Maxwell said, and stopped moving.

Five seconds later another small gray paper the size of a business card shot out of a slot next to the button. Juliana picked it up.

On the first side was the coupon for five percent off a gas purchase. Juliana turned the card over and read: "Our Fearless Leader loves kissing you, too."

"Getting a second opinion?" Diesel said from right behind her.

Juliana jumped, dropping the card, and watched as it fluttered to the floor, coupon side showing. She hadn't heard him sneak up.

Diesel bent to pick it up, but Juliana collapsed quickly to her knees and beat him to it, yanking the small card away from his fingertips.

"You can move really fast."

"Well, you can move as silent as a ninja," she said, shoving the new card into the side pocket of her purse.

"Not going to let me see it?" he asked with a devastating smile.

"Better not." She didn't want him to *know* how much she liked kissing him. But she did want to leap on him, throw him to the ground and *show* him how much she liked kissing him.

He moved closer, towering over her, his bent head putting his mouth only inches from hers. "Give me a hint."

She lifted up on her tippy toes, closing the gap between them and putting her hands on his shoulders. She felt him tense beneath her fingertips. Her cheek brushed against his sandpapery jaw as she put her mouth by his ear and whispered, "It's another coupon for five percent off my gas purchase." Juliana made contact with his jaw again, allowing his end-of-day shadow to abrade her face once more before pulling away.

He laughed, slid an arm around her shoulders and brushed his lips across hers for the barest of kisses. The desire was evident in his eyes. He moved in again. The second kiss was more serious, more engaging, more passionate, more everything. He squeezed her tight in his solid embrace and she held on for all she was worth as magical thoughts of entwining herself with him sans clothing danced wickedly in her mind.

"O Fearless Leader," a sing-song voice asked from behind them. "You're wanted at the front desk."

To his credit, Diesel didn't release her at first. He finished the kiss, pulled his lips from hers, took a half-step away and spun to face the grumpy girl from the front counter.

"Where is your nametag, Alice?" Diesel said the moment he faced the dark-haired girl.

Alice slapped a hand to her chest where the nametag would have been, but wasn't, and blushed to her roots. "I'm sorry. I forgot. I must have left it in my locker."

He nodded his head in the direction of another hallway. "Run and fetch it. But first, who wants to see me?"

"A customer," she said brightly. Alice's face was still flushed, her hand still attached to the space beneath her collarbone where her missing nametag presumably went as she stared at Diesel intently.

"Do they want to complain about something?"

"I don't think so. She seemed very happy about something and wanted to talk to the manager. I said I'd come and get you."

Diesel nodded, grabbed Juliana's hand and walked her past the clerk. Juliana had an urge to stick her tongue out at Alice, but resisted the petty gesture as immature and below her. It was tricky being an adult sometimes, when childish taunts were completely justified.

The customer in question was the one who complained about the dirty window washer container. Diesel winked at Juliana, releasing her hand with one final squeeze.

To the woman standing by the counter he said, "Hi, I'm Diesel Grey, the Fearless Leader and manager here. How can I help you?" He extended his hand. She took it wordlessly, staring at him. Then she smiled and blushed.

Juliana wondered if Diesel made every woman he met blush. He was two for two in the last couple of minutes.

Diesel released the woman's hand. She seemed

to come back to reality and said, "I just wanted you to know that the young woman behind the counter and Kenny, the young man who came outside to quickly change and refill the window washing station at the gas pumps, did so in a smooth, efficient manner. I truly appreciate it."

"Thank you so much for taking the time to let me know," Diesel said. He reached into his shirt pocket and pulled out a small business card, not unlike the one Maxwell the Martian had recently given her, wrote something on the back and handed it to her.

"This is a coupon for you. A special twenty percent off manager's code for use anywhere in the truck stop today or the next time you come in to get gas or shop. Okay?"

The woman took the card and her blank stare of surprise morphed into one of utter worship. She beamed and blushed like he'd handed her jewelry. "Thank you so much." She held it to her chest like a treasure. Juliana thought the woman was going to throw herself on Diesel's tall frame and kiss his mouth. Instead, she again thanked him profusely and eventually stumbled backward through the double swinging doors.

"Does every woman you meet fall in love with you in the first five seconds?"

Diesel spun around with surprise. "No. Why? Did you?"

Her cheeks heated to an uncomfortable level in

mere moments. Now he was three for three. "No comment," she managed.

His infectious grin warmed her. "That means yes."

She shrugged, her face still burning. "Well, you *are* very attractive. It's not a surprise when other women practically fall at your feet."

He took her back in his arms. "But I only care about what *you* think."

Juliana tried to get any look of embarrassment off her features. "Really? I do like you very much. I'm certain I'm already blushing, but I wanted to tell you that I feel like we have some sort of connection or bond. I'm hoping you feel the same way about me."

"I do feel the same way, Juliana. I haven't been able to get you out of my mind since the first time we met. That is the truth."

Diesel towered over her. She tilted her face upward. Their lips were suddenly very close yet again. He was about to kiss her, his head was moving closer. It was like they had magnetic strips embedded in their lips and every time they got close enough their mouths wanted to stick together permanently.

"O Fearless Leader?" Alice said. Juliana noticed her nametag was now perfectly in place.

"What is it?" Diesel lifted his head and turned toward Alice in one smooth move. Remarkably, he didn't even sound like he wanted to take her head off. Juliana did, though. She clamped her lips shut to keep her tongue in her mouth.

"Nova is looking for you." Alice glanced at Juliana, giving her a onceover gaze before looking at Diesel again.

Nodding, he said, "What does she want?"

Alice shrugged. "She didn't say. But it seemed important." She glanced at Juliana with a smirk, as if to say, "No more kissy-kissy for you, missy."

Diesel said, "Thanks. Next time you see her, tell her I left for the evening."

"You're leaving?" Alice seemed shocked. Her frowning gaze landed on Juliana as if she was to blame. "But...um...well, should I have her call you?"

"No. Tell her to either leave a note on my desk or get in touch with Cam. He's on duty this weekend. I won't be back until Monday morning."

Diesel grabbed Juliana's hand, not giving Alice a chance to respond or question him further. He didn't stop moving until they'd exited the convenience store, the jingle of the bell above the door heralding their departure out to the parking lot.

"Do you need to stay at work?" Juliana asked, hoping he didn't.

"Nope. I've been there long enough. One of my brothers is on duty this weekend. He can deal with whatever comes up."

"Where are we going?"

"I thought we'd go into town and search for aliens."

Chapter 10

"You're going to help me search for aliens?" Juliana asked, a quirky sweet smile shaping her lovely mouth. Diesel was so smitten.

"I thought that's what you wanted to see."

"I want to take a tour of Alienn, certainly, but I didn't expect an actual alien hunt."

"Well, I hate to disappoint you before we even get started, but I wouldn't get my hopes up that we'll actually *see* any little green aliens with red death rays shooting from their eyes."

"That's okay. I'd be delighted with a few great stories, even if they are from bygone days, that I can include in my article."

"What kind of stories?"

"I'd like to hear the kind of tale that will make folks who buy this special edition of the Finder's guide book eager to travel here to check it out so they can see it for themselves."

He pointed to his vehicle, a truck he'd had a few years. It was blue, had four-wheel-drive and was still in pretty good shape. She grinned. "I wondered what you drove."

"Oh? Why? What did you think I'd drive?"

"Honestly, I sort of expected the Fearless Leader of the Big Bang Truck Stop to drive a spacecraft or possibly a Mars rover."

He laughed. "Impractical. I'd never be able to fit either of those vehicles in my garage."

"True. And my third guess as to what you drive regularly wouldn't fit either."

"Third guess?"

"Tractor-trailer."

"Not to mention impossible to find parking anywhere I wanted to go shopping."

"However, the Fearless Leader driving a regular truck just like every third person in this state is a bit surprising."

"It's not so surprising. I told you I was an Arkansas boy. That's what we drive, trucks." He held open the passenger door for her as she climbed into his vehicle.

"Thank you. I see you're an Arkansas boy with manners."

"Well, I had a mama who insisted. Actually, come to think of it I had a daddy who did, too." He closed her door before he started kissing her like he wanted to and ended up staying in the parking lot too long.

He rounded the front of his vehicle and hopped inside, starting it up and revving the engine a couple of times. The small space in the cab already smelled deliciously like Juliana's perfume. He inhaled deeply, centered his thoughts again, and said, "Ready to go?"

"Absolutely. Let's get this tour started. I'm anxious to see what you want to show me."

Diesel nodded, having come up with a plan to show her a few things that wouldn't be terribly scandalous. She'd caught him off guard more than once. He was prepared this time. He'd done some homework after leaving her house yesterday. He'd poked around the local library for historic references to any unexplained tales that might be of interest and also had nothing to do with alien activity.

He planned to take Juliana on a tour of the small town of Alienn and point out a few places of possible curiosity that would suffice for her article, but at the same time not get him into trouble.

All history set throughout the Alphas' time here in Alienn was likely subject to a security look before release to the public, but Diesel would cross that bridge when he came to it. He was someone who believed that not all publicity was good. However, a mention in a famous travel guide like Finder's was a boon, not a scandal in the making. He hoped.

Any inclusion in this Finder's book without an actual provable alien sighting—beyond Maxwell the Martian—might bring more humans into the truck stop. He'd cite free marketing exposure as his excuse if needed, and see if he couldn't produce an uptick in sales as a result when the book was available.

Diesel pulled out of the truck stop and headed toward town. They could have walked, and if it had been a nice sunny day he might have suggested it, but it was dark. With a recently arrived spacecraft and a few extra aliens ensconced below, he didn't want to accidentally come across any strangers from another galaxy that would result in Juliana being blasted with the Defender again.

He glanced in her direction. She was looking out her passenger side window. He'd driven from her place the day before, traveling most of the way home considering his pursuit of a life with Juliana. He'd also thought about their short history and the memories she'd never get back.

She'd mentioned a dream about their experience with Maxwell the Martian, a memory the Defender should have wiped away. His first order of business upon returning home yesterday was to privately read up on the Defender for its uses, applications and capabilities to discover why it obviously hadn't worked fully on Juliana. Unless she started having more dreams about the time directly before his brother shot her with the Defender, he'd keep that volatile information close. A conversation with his security-minded brother would be a last resort.

He glanced through the notes Cam had given out when the Defender had been distributed. He wasn't able to get much useful information, just a notation that it had only failed one time, which had frustratingly not been explained in reference accompanying the device.

He'd have to do further research or ask Cam for more notes, but put it off. Cam would want to know why. Instead he moved on to his next topic of consideration: a future with Juliana. He'd never thought about marrying a human before, but after meeting Juliana and especially after kissing her, he couldn't think about anything else. He'd never thought about love at first sight, but figured that was exactly what had happened. There was no other explanation.

An Alpha marrying an earthling wasn't impossible, but it also wouldn't be easy. While there wasn't any Alpha-Prime general colonization law against it, there were strict rules and protocols that covered such an occurrence.

Surprisingly enough, not many Alphas fell in love with humans.

On the flipside, there were plenty of instances of the reverse happening. Lots of earthlings fawned over the extraterrestrial population of Alienn Arkansas, especially at the truck stop. Alphas—whether male or female—were often taller, had a more muscled physic and very symmetrical facial structures than the average human. Tall, muscular and attractive were features humans liked, apparently.

Most Alphas had long-range goals that didn't include a human mate or permanently residing on Earth. A number of Alphas only planned to stay for a few years before returning to their home planet. He equated it to serving in the military or possibly the Peace Corps for a limited time and then going back home after having lived a slightly different experience.

Even so, a handful of Alphas and humans had decided to mate over the years. It was the exception rather than the rule. In each instance, the Alpha gave up their post on Earth to move back to Alpha-Prime with their human mate. Both parties had to agree to it, in writing in fact. A blood oath was also required.

On a couple of occasions, the earthling broke up with their alien lover upon discovering the truth about Alienn, Alpha-Prime, the galactic way station, the mine and the rest.

However, the singular option for Alpha-human couples to be together was available only on Alpha-Prime, a rather barren planet by Earth standards, located far away in an adjacent galaxy. Those tragic instances of the human partners backing out were rare. The earthlings who hadn't wanted to make such a drastic location change had to be dealt with as far as their knowledge of Alienn, the Big Bang Truck Stop and especially the lower level and its galactic activities.

The most recent instance had been seven or eight years ago when Diesel's father had been Fearless Leader. They hadn't had the Defender then.

The end of that relationship had involved using the old injection recall serum to erase the entirety of the earthling's memories and allow her to reintegrate into human society, blissfully unaware of aliens hiding in plain sight in southern Arkansas.

The Alpha who'd lost his human love had been left distraught and heartbroken. He could have stayed on Earth, but not long after the breakup he'd moved back to Alpha-Prime, all alone. The recall serum didn't harm humans, but it was imprecise and sometimes erased several weeks of memories instead of only specific ones about aliens in Arkansas.

In the most recent case, the earthling had lost not only all memories of Alienn, but also the entire relationship with the Alpha she'd been ready to marry. It had been heartbreaking, but their only method to erase memories. That was well before Cam invented the handy dandy Defender. That creation was better than losing months of loving memories, but also problematic, as Diesel's experience with Juliana attested.

If Diesel continued his relationship with Juliana, he'd have to consider giving up his post as Fearless Leader and moving back to Alpha-Prime with her. Unless she refused to go and insisted on staying on

Earth. He chose to ignore that depressing and forlorn thought.

He'd been born on Earth. He had an Arkansas birth certificate and everything. So did his siblings, but they were all one hundred percent Alpha-Prime aliens. He knew no exception would be made for him because of his current title or his birthplace. It was assumed that one day he'd marry an Alpha who was either living on Earth or visiting from Alpha-Prime.

Diesel drove past the green and white flying saucer-shaped sign that listed the population of Alienn, Arkansas as 1,988.

Juliana pointed at it. "I love your flying saucer population sign. It matches your water tower."

"We had that custom made to suit our town's theme. You should have seen the look on the guy's face when we put in the request." Diesel—like his father before him—used small businesses, locally if possible or in state if not, to acquire whatever they needed. The metal fab guy a couple of counties over had also created the three-dimensional version of Maxwell hanging off the water tower. Luckily, that Maxwell had stayed put, probably because it was welded securely. It didn't hurt that it was five stories in the air.

"You should have Maxwell the Martian hanging off the side of it like on the water tower."

"We tried that years ago, but kids kept snapping it off, leaving only six little fingers on the edge of the sign. We had the metal fab guy make three replacements in a single month before the design was changed to exclude Maxwell."

"Kids will be kids, I guess."

"Honestly, adults will be adults, too." Diesel didn't think kids had snapped Maxwell off the sign. He suspected tourists. Could have been alien or human. Didn't matter, as it was the same result. So they added a smaller version of the metal population sign with Maxwell attached to their souvenir inventory for sale and made a nice tidy profit.

"Do you really have almost two thousand people in the town of Alienn? It doesn't seem that big."

"Yep. Inside the city limits of Alienn, there's a good-sized Bauxite mining operation to the west, the truck stop, of course, and the town itself." He named off all of the themed businesses close to the truck stop. "And we also sell quite a few souvenirs. We have several warehouses out east of town to store inventory to keep up with demand."

"You have a Maxwell the Martian souvenir demand?"

"He's the most popular character, but we sell all manner of alien-related merchandise."

Juliana looked at him with a quizzical expression. "Interesting."

"In fact, we have quite a healthy online business run out of the warehouses that ships direct to customers."

The number of residents included the below-ground facilities operating the way station for galactic travelers, but Diesel didn't add that to the list he rattled off for Juliana, even though about a fourth of the population worked there.

Diesel drove slowly toward the main street, past the Nebula Nail Salon. A sign in the window said, "All galactic travelers welcome!"

"I see the fun continues from the truck stop into town," she said with a smile as she stared out her window.

"Branded marketing definitely works for us." *For humans and aliens alike.*

"This is the courthouse." He pointed to a brick-and-granite building on the left. She ducked to see out his window.

"Beautiful. Is that where the infamous founder Alienne got her name shortened and never put right?"

"Yep. I'd take you inside, but it's closed for the weekend."

"Could we go in there sometime when it *is* open?"

"Sure."

Diesel continued through town until he came to a very old-fashioned building on the right. He slowed to a stop, turned off the engine and pointed out the deserted corner structure, four stories tall and painted a dull red, with a corner porch out front.

"This used to be a speakeasy back during Prohibition."

"Ooh," she said, excitedly. "I'll bet there are lots of old and very interesting stories in there."

"That's why I brought you here."

"Also it keeps the focus off the aliens at the truck stop, right?"

"Yes. You've figured out my master plan to keep the puny earthling—that would be you—from discovering our ultimate plans to take over the Earth." He smiled. "Haven't I gotten you to believe that Maxwell is the only alien in town yet?"

She shrugged. "Well, you did try to use mind control on me."

"True. And I may try again."

"Bring it," she said with a smile. "So can we get out and look around?"

"Sure. Let's go. There was an interesting story from about eighty-plus years ago that I thought you might like about an infamous duo in town and up to no good."

"That is very interesting and vague. Can we get inside and look around?"

"Maybe. Aren't you afraid?"

"Nope. Since you won't tell me about all the aliens roaming around here, I'm on the hunt for an interesting story that I can put in my article. It's really important to me to turn in something great that the book editors will love and want to include."

"You said that before. Will you share with me why this article in Finder's is so important to you?"

She opened her mouth but closed it, her body language clearly saying she was hesitant to explain, as if she feared his reaction. "It's a long story," she finally said very softly, not looking at him.

"We have all weekend."

She turned slowly and stared at him with what looked like desire. "Well, then, I'll explain sometime this weekend." She moved closer as she spoke. He leaned toward her, seeking the kiss he'd wanted when they'd gotten into his truck.

Diesel held her gaze, wanting to discuss how long she intended to stay, wanting to kiss her senseless, wanting to get lost in a sensual embrace—

Ring. Ring. Ring.

The ring of his communicator pealed loudly in the confined space of his truck cab, jarring the mutual staring contest and, worst of all, ruining the moment.

Chapter 11

"What!" Diesel growled into the device he'd pulled off his belt, easing back into the driver's seat. Juliana also leaned away from the center console, disappointed that they'd almost, but not quite, kissed.

She looked at his phone. It didn't really look like a cellular, more like a beeper. How did he have phone service here in town? Alienn must have some other way to communicate, like a closed or online system of some sort. Or perhaps it was an alien technology-based communication network ready to take over the world? Probably not. She smiled to herself and looked at him. He sure was easy to stare at.

Diesel's eyes slowly closed as he listened to the voice at the other end of the line, as if the words he heard severely disappointed him.

"I'm busy. Why can't you do it?" he asked. "Because it's my turn isn't a good enough reason, Cam. Like I said, I'm busy." He listened a little bit longer. "Never mind what I'm busy with."

She could hear a tinny voice from the other end of the phone line continue, but not what was said. "You know what? Fine. I'll do it. Stop calling me." He folded the device in half like an old flip phone and clipped it back to his belt.

"How come you have cell service?"

He looked at the phone. "Since we don't have coverage, we have a closed system we use for truck stop employees, sort of like an advanced walkie-talkie system."

"I see. I'd guessed alien technology."

"Of course you did."

She laughed. "What do you have to do that you don't want to?"

"I have to check my parents' house. They are traveling in an RV across the country. My little sister lives there, but she's out of town at some sort of summer school thing, so one of the rest of us stops by every day to ensure everything is safe and sound."

"Is this the house you grew up in?" She tried not to sound as wistful as she felt about the idea of visiting the home where he grew up with his vast number of siblings. She'd spent her entire youth wishing to be adopted into a huge family.

He nodded.

"Can I come with you?"

"Sure. Want to pop into the former speakeasy and look around first?"

"Tell me the story. What is this place besides a speakeasy?"

"The speakeasy was in the basement and rumor has it there was more than one escape route leading to tunnels that opened out in the forest yonder. But the rumored story I thought you'd be interested in was the upstairs portion, which in the early 1930s was a bank."

"There was a speakeasy in the basement of a bank?" She was dubious.

"Great cover if you ask me."

"Okay. Go on."

"So the rumor has to do with an infamous duo of bank robbers, a couple who supposedly robbed the bank."

"Infamous like Bonnie and Clyde?"

He nodded. "That's the rumor. Folks say they robbed this very bank and got away with a couple thousand dollars."

"I never heard about a Bonnie and Clyde bank robbery in this area. They only robbed some places in western Arkansas, right?"

"Supposedly this robbery didn't ever make it into the papers." His smile said there was more to the story.

"Why?" she asked, playing along.

"The rumor was that the bank owner himself let them inside that day. He was also the one who opened the safe. So after this infamous bank robber couple left, he covered the whole thing up and never even called the police."

"Really." This was a great story.

"The bank manager and the two tellers working there that day were threatened not to reveal the truth. He apparently forced them to sign some early form of non-disclosure agreement to frighten them into keeping quiet."

"So who ended up telling the secret?"

Diesel grinned. "The bank owner confessed on his deathbed at the ripe old age of ninety-four."

"Hmm. That *is* interesting."

"There are those who believe they saw Bonnie and Clyde in the basement speakeasy a couple of nights in a row before allegedly robbing the bank."

"Oh?"

"You know, casing the joint for their big robbery."

"Any way to prove that?"

"Well, I can prove they were in the speakeasy, but I can't prove they robbed the bank."

"What's the proof?"

"A picture taken of them at the bar without their knowledge."

"Is that so?"

"It is."

"Where is the picture?"

"In the courthouse."

"So that means I'll have to come back on Monday to see the proof, right?"

"That's one option." He started his truck and drove away from the former bank and speakeasy.

"Let me run by and check my folks' house and then I'll take you back to my place for dinner. We can discuss any and all plans, okay?"

"Perfect."

He drove to a large, beautiful brick home with front wrap-around porch and a long driveway leading to a huge backyard and a detached four-car garage. He pulled around to the back of the house and opened his door. "I won't be long."

"Can I come with you?"

He tilted his head to one side. "You want to see inside?"

"I'd like to see your childhood home, yes."

He held up his hand signaling her to wait. She thought he was abandoning her until he rounded the front of his truck and opened her door. She'd forgotten about his ingrained manners.

"Come along, then. I'll give you the nickel tour." He held her hand as she stepped down from his truck.

At the back door was a key pad. He put his hand flat on it and then entered a long code. The door clicked open.

"Top-notch security, I see."

"Yeah. They probably don't need it, but Cam insists."

There was a light on over the stove as she stepped into the large country kitchen. The faint scent of coffee filled the air. She looked to her right and saw a coffee maker on the counter. He entered right behind her and locked the deadbolt on the kitchen door behind them.

"Will you show me your old room?"

"Ah. Sure. It's a converted attic space on the third floor."

She nodded, even though he mentioned the location like it was an undesirable place to visit.

He took her hand, kissed the tips of her fingers and led her through the kitchen. "This is the kitchen," he said.

"I see."

"It's all a part of the nickel tour."

"What if I don't have a nickel?"

"I'll require a kiss at the end of the tour then."

"Deal."

From the kitchen, they moved into a large dining room with a lovely table big enough to seat twelve comfortably. She easily pictured a family of nine, mostly boys, and the image tugged at her heart a bit.

Next they rounded the table and went through another archway to the foyer. He guided her to a staircase leading up to the second floor. They climbed the steps together, turning left down a hallway at the top. As they walked along—and as he'd done downstairs—he pointed to the first partly open door on the left to announce what it was. "This is my little sister's room." Further down on the right there were two more doors to rooms that had been shared by four of his brothers. "Jack and Gage were in one room. They were the two youngest. And the other had Axel and Wheeler."

"Don't you have five brothers? One named Cam, right?"

He nodded. "Yep. But when Cam turned twelve, he decided three boys sharing one bedroom had two too many boys in it, so my parents fixed him up a small space over the garage where an ancient efficiency apartment used to be."

At the end of the hallway was another door. He opened it, flipped a light switch on and revealed a narrow staircase leading to the third floor.

"Up there is where I was."

"You got your own room?"

He nodded. "While it's a good-sized space up there, it's mostly unfinished, just wood and beams."

"Can we go up and look at it?"

Diesel tilted his head once, gesturing her to follow him. She couldn't help but watch his backside as he climbed. He really filled out a pair of jeans well.

The staircase was short, leading to a small landing, another turn to the right and they climbed the rest of the way into the attic space. A small railing at the top opened into darkness. Diesel turned the light on just as she got to eye level with the attic space. She saw his massive bed first. Her heart skipped a beat for some reason.

Juliana climbed the rest of the stairs and went to stand next to him in the middle of the room.

"What do you think?"

She walked over to the king bed and sat down at the foot of the mattress. His eyes widened. "I like it," she said, looking into his surprised gaze. She smoothed her hands over the colorful quilt atop the bed and then patted the space beside her. "Join me."

He cleared his throat and crossed to sit next to her, his thigh pressing against hers as he got comfortable. Diesel took her hand and kissed her fingertips once more. He pushed out a long sigh as if trying to decide whether to grant her fondest wish or pretend her motives weren't of the wicked variety.

Juliana didn't want her intentions to be misread. She turned toward him, wrapped an arm around his neck and kissed his mouth hard and deep to ensure he knew *exactly* what she wanted.

When she pulled him down so they were both parallel to the surface of the bed, he broke the kiss and stared deeply, passionately into her eyes. The look she saw solidified the idea that he'd figured out what she was after. His next eager kiss told her he wanted the exact same thing.

Diesel woke up slowly the next morning. Before he even opened his eyes, the sluggishness in his entire body was conspicuous. He didn't feel bad or like he was getting sick, but something was very different.

He was face down on his belly, just as he normally slept, but when he managed to crack open an eyelid, he didn't see his bedroom. Both eyes popped opened wider as he tried to figure out where he was. The space was both familiar and alien, and yet not the master bedroom in his home.

Where am I?

He saw the stairs leading into the attic space of his former bedroom, and then a whole rush of important memories shot into his brain like a cannon blast of information.

Last night. Juliana. Magical.

He couldn't even think in full sentences. A flood of images and memories overwhelmed him, at least making him wake up faster. He lifted to his elbows, searching the bed for Juliana, but he was alone. He looked to where he knew he'd tossed Juliana's shirt last night, but it wasn't there.

Where is she?

Diesel climbed out of bed, searching every corner of the room. She was not here. He looked inside the small bathroom, but she wasn't there either. He retrieved his clothing—strewn about the room during last night's captivating events—and put yesterday's outfit back on along with his boots. As he tied the final lace into a bow and tucked them into the ties, he heard a noise downstairs in the area of the kitchen.

The scent of coffee wafted its way upstairs to tease him with the desire to follow the trail and find some caffeine goodness.

Juliana was seated on a stool at the end of the kitchen island near the coffee pot. Her hands were wrapped around a steaming cup and she sipped the edge carefully. More images from the night before flashed in his brain. Juliana was extraordinary.

"Did you save any for me?" he asked, hoping not to startle her.

She didn't jump. Her gaze slowly lifted to where he stood in the doorway. She smiled the moment she saw him.

Nodding, she said, "I did. I made a whole pot. I hope you don't mind me rummaging around in here."

"Nope. I appreciate it."

"I really can't function well until I've had at least one cup." She took another careful sip and sighed out loud in apparent bliss.

"We have that in common," Diesel said. He strode over to the cupboard with the mugs, snagged a large one and poured himself a cup that looked hot and strong, just the way he liked it. He took a quick mouth-burning sip to get some caffeine into his system and seated himself across from her on another stool at the kitchen island.

They peered over their coffee cups at each other. He smiled. She smiled back.

Diesel wasn't sure what to say. His sleep-muddled brain made the smart decision not to speak until the connection to his mouth was better established.

She nodded at his mug. "Does it taste okay?"

"Perfect." They each took another sip. His stomach was about to make a noise and he remembered something he'd forgotten to do the night before.

"It just now occurs to me that I never made you dinner last night. I'm a terrible host. My belly is about to rumble. You must be starving."

A wistful smile shaped her lips. "You aren't a terrible host. What we did last night was way better than dinner and we did share three incredible courses."

Diesel grinned. He reached out and brushed his fingertips over one of her hands, which was still wrapped around her coffee mug. "You're right. All three courses were truly spectacular. But my stomach is about to make a really ugly noise."

"When I was looking for coffee, I also searched around a bit in here. I'm afraid it's slim pickings. And my stomach noise may rival yours."

Diesel went to the pantry and came back with a box of granola bars. "Here is something to tide us over until I can make real food."

They each unwrapped a bar, taking large bites. "What are you going to make?" she asked and took another big bite of granola bar.

"Pancakes," he managed around his own second mouthful. "I'll cook and you can share with me why writing the article for this book is so important."

"Okay. Point me to the right cupboards and I'll gather some plates and forks." He opened the correct cabinet for her and pointed to the drawer with the silverware.

Diesel found a skillet in the cupboard next to the stove, mixed some batter that only needed to have water added. After setting their places, she resumed her seat and sipped her coffee.

"As I mentioned before, I was left on the doorstep of a church in Washington State. I grew up in an orphanage nearby."

"I remember."

"I had absolutely no notion of who my family was or where I'd come from. Still don't. When I left to go to college in Missouri, I kept in touch with one of the ladies who ran the orphanage, Miss Hester. When she passed away last year, an envelope was sent to me with a note indicating Miss Hester had saved the contents for me.

"It was mostly pictures of me growing up. I'd seen most of them before, but there was one of me as a baby that I hadn't. On the back of the picture was written, *abandoned baby* and the date."

"Was it a different date than you thought?" he asked. "It would be cool to find out you were younger, right?"

She smiled. "No. The date was right. I'm twenty-six, there's no getting around that."

"You're a young thing. I'm thirty, in case you wanted to know. But keep going, sorry to interrupt." He flipped the last pancake on the plate and turned the heat off the skillet. He grabbed some butter and syrup along with the plate of pancakes.

"The picture itself was of a baby in an oval woven basket. But there was also a blanket with three initials, JEM, on one corner."

"JEM? Juliana, middle initial that starts with E and last name Masters?"

"Yes. I believe so."

"What's your middle name?"

"Elizabeth. What's yours?"

He pushed out a long sigh. "All of us boys have our father's name as our middle name."

"And what's your father's name?"

"Zebulon."

She smiled, ate a few bites of buttermilk pancake and said, "These are great."

"Thanks. So you want to go back and find the blanket, hoping it will lead you to information about your missing family."

"Well, yes. But also shown in the picture was what looked like a small book or maybe even a journal. That's what I'm truly after."

"Why wouldn't they have given it to you?"

"The orphanage was what they liked to think of as forward thinking. They operated under the idea that however children ended up there, we were better off and should look to make our own futures and not dwell on the past. There is always the possibility it was a small bible or something from the orphanage, but I want to check it out regardless."

"I don't blame you for wanting to go back."

"The article will pay enough to fund a trip so I can go back for a few weeks to look around and research. I'd love to find out if I have any family. I'd understand about them leaving me at an orphanage if they hadn't been able to care for me. I didn't have a bad upbringing."

Diesel almost told her about his cousin Stella, who had a similar story of life in an orphanage, albeit a galaxy away. He actually started out with the words, "My cousin Stella..." but didn't finish his sentence, because how would he explain that Stella came from Alpha-Prime, a planet in another galaxy, without making up a story—lie—he'd have to remember?

Instead, he shoveled a pile of butter- and syrup-laden pancake in his mouth. How horrible for him would it be for Juliana to discover a long-lost family in Washington State, and promptly leave Arkansas forever? Diesel considered their newly entwined relationship.

After he swallowed the big mouthful, he said, "Maybe I could go with you, whenever you travel back to the northwest."

"Why?"

"Because I don't think I can live without you for a day, let alone a few weeks, especially after last night."

"And here I thought you were just being polite after a night you obviously didn't expect."

He'd started to say something about his cousin Stella, but didn't finish. Then he surprised her by being very forward about his feelings.

He grabbed her hand as if afraid she'd run if he got too personal. "Make no mistake, Juliana Elizabeth Masters. I'm not being polite because last night was unexpected. And to be honest, while it was certainly unforeseen, I don't have any doubts about what I want going forward. I care deeply about you. I have since the moment we met."

Juliana was relieved. Last night had been, in a word, magical. She'd been drawn to him the first time she'd laid eyes on him. Now that they'd been intimate her feelings were even more entangled, not with whether they'd have a future, but what it would consist of. She hadn't planned on staying in this area. Even Miss Penny thought she should go back and try to find her lost family in Washington State.

"The thing is, I don't want you to get the wrong impression of me." She gazed into his beautiful blue eyes. "I don't usually...you know." Her cheeks heated, but she didn't care. He didn't comment or smirk. He looked relieved and gave her a devastatingly gorgeous grin.

He squeezed her hand. "I know. Me neither."

"Really? You don't have a whole posse of women chasing after you, tossing room keys and underwear at you to lure your attentions their way?" *Like a rock star.* He definitely had rock star looks or maybe even movie star looks.

He made a face, laughing at the implication. "Nope. Not even close."

"Even though every female you meet blushes her way through the first few seconds of any introduction, falling instantly in love with you."

He shrugged as a half-smile shaped his lips. "All I can tell you is that I've never been interested in anyone like that until you came along."

"What about the whole apple with the bite taken out problem?"

He shook his head slightly as if hating to be reminded of it. "I'm not certain what that's about, but if someone is after me, it's one sided. I don't know who it is, but once I find out I'll ensure they know I'm spoken for."

"So until this unknown entity understands your feelings," Juliana immediately thought of Alice and her poor attitude, "should I be worried?"

"I promise I won't let anything happen to you."

Diesel abandoned his empty pancake plate and

moved to the stool right beside her. He scooted that stool closer, leaned in, hooked an arm around her neck and kissed her soundly. It was a passionate kiss, a deeply satisfying kiss. The kind of kiss that was about to lead back to his childhood bedroom for a duplication of last night's magical affair.

At least until his phone rang and startled them apart. He rolled his eyes and gave his phone a stare that could melt metal. Juliana kissed his cheek and said, "Answer it. I don't want to keep the Fearless Leader from his responsibilities."

"I'm off this weekend. Whoever it is can just suck it." The ringing stopped and then started up again seconds later as they stared at each other, her with general amusement, him with long-suffering exasperation.

Juliana laughed. "Answer it. Tell them you're busy."

"They know I'm busy. I'm afraid it will be some earth-shattering emergency that will force me to go into the office to solve it. Like my aunt Dixie has decided to streak naked through town for some ridiculous money-making scheme she's concocted in my short absence."

"I could go with you."

He looked her over from the top to bottom, shaking his head. "You look sleep rumpled and far too delicious. I don't want anyone else to see you looking so amazingly good."

"Well, I feel the same way about you." She

smoothed a hand down her hair, feeling like it was probably standing on end. "I don't suppose we could shower before you have to go solve all of your aunt's public nudity issues."

"Possibly."

Diesel's phone started ringing for the third time after only a couple of seconds of silence. He pulled his walkie-talkie-like device off his belt, opened it up and said, "This better be life or death with bloodshed involved."

He listened and his brows immediately furrowed. He closed his eyes, pushed out a long sigh and said, "I'll be there as soon as I can."

At the other end of the line, Juliana thought she heard someone say, "No! Now!"

"See you soon," Diesel said and snapped his phone shut.

"We'll have to do quick showers. I do need to go take care of something." He looked distracted, as if his mind was already on the problem he faced at work. He led her back upstairs and into his sister's room. It had its own bathroom. "You can use Valene's bathroom. She won't mind. She's about your size, although a bit taller, if you want to borrow some of her clothes."

"Thanks. I actually packed a bag, just in case, but my car is still parked at the truck stop."

He nodded. "That's okay. Valene really won't care if you borrow something. I'll meet you downstairs in the foyer when you're done."

Juliana took the fastest shower she'd ever taken, pulled her hair into a half ponytail-half bun hairdo, and found a gray T-shirt with a bright green Big Bang Truck Stop logo and a pair of denim capris in Valene's closet that fit Juliana like regular jeans. She met Diesel in the foyer in fifteen minutes flat, her personal best.

He looked relieved when she descended the stairs, but they didn't linger. Five minutes later they were halfway to the truck stop.

Once he parked his truck in the same spot as last night, he came around and opened her door for her.

"I won't be too long. Do you mind hanging out in the convenience store? Or do you want to meet me at the Cosmos Café?"

"I'll wait for you in the store. I'm full of pancakes."

He grabbed her hand and together they walked to the front of the store and inside.

Alice was at the register again. Her sour expression when she saw Juliana changed the moment Diesel stepped through the door behind her.

"Good morning, Fearless Leader," Alice said exuberantly.

"Good morning." He gestured to Juliana. "Anything she wants, put on my tab and I'll settle up when I return."

Alice's smile dimmed only momentarily. "Of course, whatever she wants."

Diesel squeezed Juliana's hand once, lifting it to his lips. "I have an employee dispute to resolve, but it shouldn't take too long. I'll try to hurry, okay?"

"Okay."

He gave her a lusty gaze and kissed her fingertips gently. The gesture was so touching she wanted to wrap her whole self around this man and keep him forever.

"I'll wait right here."

"Perfect." Diesel kissed her hard and fast on the mouth before walking away toward his office. She watched him go as the taste of him lingered on her lips. Hoo boy, he was something else. When he was gone from her sight, an icy chill rushed through her body from deep inside outward to her limbs. Like a reverse hot flash maybe.

Juliana happened to glance over her shoulder at Alice, whose shocked expression changed once Diesel was out of view. She'd probably sent a mental ice bucket to pour on Juliana's head.

The clerk cleared her throat and said, "Are you going to want something or not?" Her tone and attitude had gone from syrupy with Diesel to snotty with her. Juliana didn't care.

The night they'd spent together cemented her feelings, and Diesel seemed very serious about wanting her in his future. Alice or anyone else who fancied themselves in love with Diesel could suck it. She smiled thinking about Diesel using that same reference.

"I don't know. Maybe I'll take a look around."

She noticed a basket of fresh fruit on the counter, seeing both bananas and apples. On the spur of the moment, she walked over, picked out the largest apple and held it up to Alice. "Listen up. I know what you're doing, but hear me when I say you're wasting your time. And stop with the apples. It's not going to change anything I do and it's wasteful."

Alice's eyes widened to the size of saucers. "I'm sure I don't know what you're talking about."

"Oh? Don't you?" Juliana put the apple back in the basket and walked away. She wandered down the main aisle toward the back of the store, not intending to go all the way to Diesel's office, but just closer to where she knew he was, hoping it would help warm her sudden cold snap.

She missed him the moment he'd stepped away, like physically being ripped away from his immediate presence had caused this lingering cold within. What was that about?

Diesel returned as if conjured by her desire for him, and gave her a look like he was a man in love. Juliana shivered.

"Are you cold?"

"Yep. The moment you walked away it was like a frigid chill washed over me." The icy air had certainly come from Alice the moment he was out of her sight.

He wrapped his arms around her, warming her

instantly. "This dispute might take longer than I thought. Do you want to wait in my office? Or I can give you the keys to my truck."

"I appreciate the sacrifice of offering to let me drive your truck. I understand most Arkansas boys flinch at the mere prospect." He shrugged and tightened his grip. "But my car is still parked out there. I'll just wait in your office, if that's okay."

They were standing well inside the convenience store, but also within view of Alice, the snotty clerk.

The way Diesel looked at her was impossible to miss. Alice didn't miss it, either. Juliana saw her surprise. The anger had seemingly gone out of her. She didn't smile, exactly, but she nodded once in their direction as if acknowledging Diesel was, for now, Juliana's.

Interesting.

"Come on. I'll show you my office."

"Can't wait."

He took Juliana's hand and moved toward the back of the store. She liked that he seemed to want to keep touching her as he led her around the convenience store like his date at a party.

Behind them the bell on the convenience store doors rang three times in quick succession. Presumably it meant that if Alice hadn't caught them canoodling, then there were about to be three more opportunities to be interrupted from customers coming inside. This sparked an unreasonable flash of anger.

Unreasonable because this was his workplace and not Lover's Lane. Juliana needed to be more cautious about kissing him whenever the desire emerged—which was every single second in his presence—instead of giving in to her unparalleled attraction in public.

Diesel led her past Maxwell the Martian, down the hallway and past his receptionist's desk to his office. A door labeled Our Fearless Leader was ajar, and someone stood on the threshold.

"Cam," Diesel said, not relinquishing her hand as he pushed past his brother and skirted the outer edge of the desk.

Juliana looked at Cam, noticing what looked like a miniature blue and white megaphone hooked on his belt. She had a flash of memory so strong she staggered against Diesel.

"Are you okay?" he asked.

Juliana stared into his eyes but only saw a recent dream she'd had, and recited the memory out loud. "I dreamed that I saw a half octopus-half man creature heading for the basement of this place."

Turning toward Cam, she pointed at the small megaphone. "And then he came along and pointed that bullhorn at me until I fell asleep."

Chapter 12

Diesel watched Cam's expression carefully as he quickly positioned himself in front of Juliana.

Cam snagged the Defender from his belt, just as Diesel expected.

"Don't, Cam," he said. "Obviously it doesn't work on her."

"It did at first. Step out of the way."

"No. I don't want you to shoot her. She remembers what happened as if it was a dream."

"That's impossible."

"You just heard her for yourself."

"What is going on here?" Juliana asked, her voice wavering and fearful. "That *was* a dream. Wasn't it?"

Diesel gave Cam a look that said he'd better behave and turned away. The moment he did, Cam aimed the Defender at Juliana and shot her again.

Her eyes closed. She crumpled like paper, heading straight toward the floor until Diesel caught her and lifted her into his arms.

"I told you not to do that! What is wrong with you?"

"We need to study her and find out how she can remember. She shouldn't be able to."

"No. We don't. She's not some guinea pig you can experiment on in your basement laboratory."

His brother frowned. "They were gerbils and none of them were ever hurt in any way."

"No, Cam. You may not study her. That is my final answer!"

Cam approached, lifting one of her eyelids and looking at her pupil as if he hadn't heard Diesel's command. "How else will we find out how she can remember stuff after being shot?"

"I don't care why." Diesel yanked her away from Cam, who'd already put a thumb on her chin, trying to look inside her mouth. "Maybe she's special."

Cam huffed, crossing his arms in annoyance when Diesel backed out of his reach. "You should care about the security of our species hiding on this planet, O Fearless Leader. Why are you being so difficult?"

Diesel stared down into Juliana's passive sleeping expression. "I care about her." He remembered last night. "I'm also involved with her. In fact, I'm falling in love with her."

Cam's frown deepened. "You can't get involved with an earthling."

"Too late." Diesel kissed her temple. The sweet

scent of her skin warmed him to his bones as he held her. She was the one. The *only* one for him. He knew it as surely as he was standing here.

"But you have an arranged marriage to fulfill one of these days."

"No. I don't. It doesn't have to be me. Why don't *you* fulfill it?"

"I don't want a wife here on Earth."

"Perfect. The wife from your arranged marriage can live on Alpha-Prime and you can stay on Earth and fulfill that edict easily, because it's not going to be me." He lifted Juliana higher in his arms and kissed her cheek, wondering how long she'd stay asleep this time.

Axel came into the room. "What are you two fighting about?" His eyes landed on Juliana. "Who's that?"

"Juliana," Diesel and Cam said. His Security Officer then added, "And the human our eldest brother is stupid over."

Axel nodded. "Awesome. She's pretty. Good for you. There is someone here who wants to talk to you."

Diesel pushed out a long sound of displeasure, remembering the woman from the night before. "It's not some truck stop customer gushing about the window washer water being perfect, is it?"

Axel squinted. "Uh, no. This is from downstairs." He eyed Juliana. "Know what I mean?"

"Got it. I'm just a little busy right now." Diesel tightened his grip on Juliana as if he needed to protect her. "I'm already refereeing a dispute between two graveyard shift employees, threatening to quit."

Axel eyed Juliana again. "Bummer. And yet still, I need you to meet someone."

"Who is it?"

"You know the representative from the Royal Caldera Cruise Line ship that came in last night?"

"No. You didn't mention there was any representative aboard."

"Oh. Sorry. There was a Royal Caldera Cruise Line representative aboard the most recent...arrival. He came in on last night's transport. He just told me he needs to meet with you."

"Now?"

Axel looked at Juliana and then at Cam—who still had his Defender in hand, ready to shoot it again—and finally seemed to figure out what was going on. "Did you shoot Diesel's human girlfriend with a Defender?"

"He doesn't need a human girlfriend," Cam said after a few seconds' pause.

Axel snapped his fingers. "Oh, right. I forgot you volunteered to be Diesel's mother while Mom is away RVing with Dad."

Cam frowned and Diesel figured there was a fight brewing. He said, "Enough. Settle down, the two of you. Axel, tell the representative I'm unable to meet with him right now or today at all. Ask if Monday morning at ten will work. Also, step into the conference room and tell the two employees there that I've been called away. I'll talk to them on Monday."

"Sure thing." He shaped his fingers and thumbs like guns and pointed them at Cam, making a soft, "Pew, pew," noise, blowing on the tips of his index fingers as if they were still smoking after he was done.

Cam did not look amused as Axel left the office.

"How long was the Defender set for, Cam? And keep in mind that if you're about to tell me the maximum of thirty minutes, I don't know that I'll be able to keep from grabbing it out of your hand and beating you with it."

Cam looked down at the dial. "It wasn't the maximum. It was only set for ten minutes. Are you happy?"

"No. I'm far from happy." Diesel looked at the clock on his wall. I don't think she's been here for ten minutes yet."

"Yes, she has. Ten minutes and forty seconds since you both came in. We can still put her back in your truck and—"

"No."

"What do you mean, no? She will remember getting here—"

"And what? Falling asleep in my truck yet again

upon arriving in our parking lot? Don't you think she might eventually wonder why she pulls into this truck stop and immediately becomes unconscious?"

"I don't care. The humans can make up whatever story helps them understand their circumstances."

Juliana's eyes fluttered and he felt her muscles tense. She was waking up.

Cam lifted his Defender.

"Do. Not. Even." Diesel walked to the small sofa in his office and seated himself there with Juliana on his lap. "Leave us. Now."

Cam opened his mouth to argue, but Diesel gave him a brotherly death stare to ensure he understood his passion in this matter. "Now," he repeated.

His brother huffed, but turned and left his office, slamming the door hard enough that it rattled in the frame. He didn't care if Cam was mad. He'd crossed the line.

Diesel twisted and sat Juliana up beside him on the sofa. Her head lolled on his shoulder. Diesel brushed a lock of hair away from her eyes, running his palm along her cheek. She was so soft. So beautiful. So perfect.

"Have I mentioned that I'm really glad you're here, Juliana?" He leaned closer to brush his mouth over hers. She responded to his kiss, surprisingly enough.

"I had planned to fall madly in love with you," he whispered, breaking the kiss only long enough to tell her how he felt. He wanted to try out loud the words he'd been thinking, wondering if she'd remember and hoping she felt the same way about him. "The truth is, I'm already madly in love with you."

"What?" she asked in a soft voice.

He repeated what he'd said, adding, "Are you ready for a further tour of the township of Alienn?"

She glanced around his office cautiously. She looked as sleep rumpled and tempting as she had this morning at the kitchen island. He didn't know how he'd ever live without her in his life. He was certain he didn't want to attempt it.

"How did I get in here?"

"We walked in. Don't you remember?"

Diesel had never been more certain of anything in his life beyond wanting command of this facility. He'd wanted to be in charge and he enjoyed his role as Fearless Leader. He also wanted Juliana to be his forever. She warmed him all the way to his bones whenever they were together.

Juliana put her palm on his chest. "Even after only one night together, you've already fallen madly in love with me?"

"Yes. Exactly." *I want to make you mine forever.* Then we can take a real tour, or better yet, a honeymoon.

She lifted her head from his shoulder and stared

deeply into his eyes, her soft, sleepy gaze filling him with an emotion he hadn't ever felt before. His soul melted when she was nearby. He already *had* fallen in love with her, would always love her. He couldn't imagine spending another day without her permanently by his side.

Her gaze never wavered. "I've decided that I'll fall madly in love with you, too."

"Perfect." He lowered his head, kissing her softly and thoroughly.

At least until there was a quiet knock at his office door, breaking their kiss and sending the level of his ire into the sky. They were busy falling madly in love with one another. Interruptions were more than bothersome. He'd always considered himself even tempered, but the mad love of one beautiful earthling had opened up a wide range of passionate emotions.

"What!" he shouted at the door.

Axel opened the door cautiously and slowly, grinning when he noticed Juliana was awake. "Really sorry to intrude, Bro, but the…uh…you know, the representative from the…uh…travel line?"

"Yes, I remember. I suggested meeting on Monday instead of today." Diesel also remembered his typical Sundays and how unbelievably busy they were. He was always utterly alone, but rarely got any work in his office completed, which was why he'd wanted to take last night and today off and stay away.

Diesel wanted to show Juliana his office and then his home. They'd spent the night in his childhood home, so she hadn't even seen his house yet. It was on a cul-de-sac, but his home was centered on two lots, giving him lots of space in front.

He wanted to show her everything that was important in his life. He wanted to discover if she would relish the simple pleasures he enjoyed. Like his screened-in back porch with the tranquil view of a pond and the wall of trees beyond the water's far edge, leading to a vast, dense forest.

If he'd wanted privacy he could have taken her immediately to his home, but often his life was not his own. He had lots of surprise chores because he was part of a large family. He'd never noticed before because he'd never had a girlfriend before. An unreasonable goofy feeling swelled as he thought the word "girlfriend."

Not that the interruption level in his ordinary life would be lower at his place or his parents' house, but at least when he wasn't at the truck stop, Cam wouldn't be racing around shooting his Defender off every five seconds and making Diesel's love life more complicated.

Axel glanced at Juliana and said, "The representative can't meet tomorrow at ten. As a matter of fact, he'd like to meet with you right now."

"Too bad. I'm busy right now. Why don't you

represent me this time? Take him and show him whatever he wants to see. You'll have fun."

Axel's hands went up in a conciliatory gesture. "If I could, I would. Trust me, I already tried that, but he's rather insistent that it needs to be you and he wants to meet," Axel looked down at his watch, "well, about five minutes ago." His brother's sheepish grin told Diesel that at least Axel was on his side with regard to Juliana. He also wouldn't have interrupted or called him here without cause.

Diesel stood and left a very quiet Juliana seated on his sofa. She didn't quite seem awake yet. That might help later on with the doozy of an explanation he'd have to render. They'd driven here and then somehow she'd made it into his office without remembering how she got there.

"What is this guy's problem anyway? Nothing is scheduled on the books for a meeting today. He can reshape his request to *my* schedule. And today, especially now, is not a good time for me."

Before Axel could say another word, a man in the rather unusual Royal Caldera Cruise Line uniform—definitely constructed from fabric not of this world—pushed Axel aside and marched into Diesel's office, looking rather perturbed. There were rules about those below coming up without an invitation. Diesel was about to inform this man he'd broken all of them.

"My problem, O Fearless Leader, is that I'm not a representative for the Royal Caldera Cruise Line.

I'm an inspector for Royal Caldera. I'm here to conduct a surprise examination of the premises, including all of the facilities."

Juliana asked in a very confused voice, "You have cruise lines coming here to the truck stop? Like big boats? How odd."

Juliana stood up and her attention immediately focused on the unusual material of the man's uniform. It was made of a popular Alpha-Prime manufactured display fabric. The back of his suit jacket could show a live television broadcast or emergency information in the event of an accident.

The outer part of the uniform could also be programmed, like it was now, to display images like a 3-D kaleidoscope of swirling shapes morphing into small dots, breaking apart and blowing around his jacket like the screen saver display on a computer.

Juliana's eyes fixed on the inspector's jacket. "What kind of material is that?"

The inspector frowned. "Alpha-Prime standard spacecraft uniform fabric. Why?"

Juliana's eyes narrowed. "What is Alpha-Prime?"

Chapter 13

Alpha-Prime sounded like an online service that would be top notch at everything it did. After asking what it was, she didn't care if she found out. What was wrong with her?

Juliana's brain felt extra foggy as she stared at the vibrant fabric. The material looked like it was alive. She blinked a couple of times, staring at the unusual jacket. She couldn't seem to focus.

It was like most mornings she lived. She typically couldn't form sentences until her first cup of coffee. But she'd already had two cups of coffee this morning, hadn't she? One cup before he made pancakes and one during the meal.

She remembered last night, vividly. She remembered this morning equally well. Juliana even remembered that she was wearing clothes borrowed from Diesel's sister. But how had she managed to doze off after arriving at the truck stop? She had not even a shred of memory as to how she'd made it into this room.

"Is this your office, Diesel?" she asked,

momentarily forgetting about the strange fabric the intense inspector wore. "How did we get here? I don't exactly remember."

The man with the strange suit looked at her like she was an alien after asking about Alpha-Prime, whatever that was, and like she was drunk for asking how she'd gotten into Diesel's office.

Her eyes slid shut, wanting to remain that way, but she blinked them open. A quick glance around the room yielded no kind of mirror. She hoped her hair wasn't standing up on end or mussed like she'd been rolling around kissing Diesel for a good long while on his comfy sofa. Then again, she couldn't remember that very well either. Is that what they'd just been doing? Was she so far gone from his kisses she couldn't remember recent events? Given that they were falling madly in love with each other, she guessed it was possible. But certainly curious.

She'd woken up a few minutes ago in the middle of kissing Diesel with no recollection of how she'd gotten all the way from the truck stop's parking lot to a room inside the building.

The third man in the room, presumably Diesel's brother, although she'd never met him before, looked very uncomfortable.

"Is this woman an earthling? She shouldn't be in your office. Isn't this private?" asked the inspector with the interesting animated shirt.

"Yes. She is. And, yes, it's private. However, I

invited her into my office," Diesel said. "You, on the other hand, just barged in here. You are supposed to remain below."

"Be that as it may, if you want this galactic way station to be a regular and continuing part of the Royal Caldera Cruise Line port of call, you'll cooperate. As an inspector I have more leeway regarding rules." The man puffed up a bit, acting like he was important and not being treated as his obvious superior station should be handled.

Diesel opened his mouth, looking rather annoyed, but the man Juliana presumed to be his brother said, "Inspector Centauri, why don't we leave and let Our Fearless Leader wrap up his meeting? I'll take you to get a bite to eat." He reached for the man's arm as if to guide him out of the office.

The man yanked his arm away and said, "No. This is a surprise assessment. Once I announce my purpose, the inspection must commence immediately."

"Okay. Diesel, why don't you go with Inspector Centauri and I'll take—" he stared at Juliana. "I'm sorry, what was your name?"

She didn't get a chance to answer.

"Juliana," Diesel said. Then he added, "Juliana, this is my brother, Axel."

She nodded once and extended her hand to Axel. "Pleased to meet you."

"Likewise. And I'm super sorry to interrupt

your date," he said softly, and turned to Diesel. "Want me to take her to your place?"

Diesel looked at her like he was being forced to do something he didn't want to. She answered for him. "Yes. He can take me to your house and I'll wait there until your inspection is complete."

Diesel took her hand. "I'm sorry our day has been interrupted. I'll try to wrap this up as fast as I can, okay?"

She nodded.

"I'd planned a more detailed tour of the town and then dinner at my place. You know, the one we never got to eat last night."

She grinned. "I do remember last night." She squeezed his fingers gently. "Don't worry. I also remember well that my neighbor interrupted us, breaking up our last date at my place." She tilted her head to one side. "You don't think it's the universe trying to tell us something, do you?"

"No. I don't. The universe is a busy enough without concern for our new relationship. Axel will take you to my house and I'll be there directly."

"Okay." Juliana smiled at Axel. He seemed to be the easy-going brother. Not like... Cam, was it? He was definitely the grumpy brother. The names in this family were very interesting. Then again, what did she expect from a family running a semi-famous truck stop in southern Arkansas?

"Make sure you take her out through the public

door," Diesel said in a low tone to Axel. "Do you want the keys to my truck?"

Juliana said, "Is your home close enough to walk to? I feel like I need to stretch a little and wake up more."

"Sure thing, we can walk there," Axel said. "And don't worry. I've got your back, Bro."

"I know you do. And if you can avoid Cam on your way to my house, that would be great."

Axel winked at him and nodded once. Taking Juliana's elbow, Axel said, "Happy inspecting. I'll return directly."

Inspector Centauri pushed out a long-suffering sigh. "Can we go now?" he asked in a tone much like one coming from the backseat during a long road trip. He stared at the wall clock like he was severely pressed for time.

"Juliana," Diesel said. She turned toward him and he gave her a look that made her melty inside. "I won't be too long."

"It's fine. Do what you need to and I'll be waiting for you." He looked like he wanted to kiss her goodbye, but Inspector Centauri started tapping the screen of an electronic clipboard she hadn't noticed him carrying and asking questions about accommodations and the level of amenities available for the wealthy guests aboard Royal Caldera Cruise Line ships, citing that they demanded the very best.

She didn't hear Diesel's response, but hopefully

he'd be more cordial once she was gone. She didn't want him to lose business because of her.

Axel led her toward the front of the convenience store, meaning they'd have to pass by Alice. Juliana decided to take the high road, not wanting to tempt or give reason to the possibility that the universe didn't want them together for some reason.

If Alice was jealous she was dating Diesel, too bad. Alice frowned when she saw Juliana, until she noticed Axel walking alongside her. Her expression softened.

As they got a couple of steps away from the counter, Juliana asked, "Do you want to simply give me directions to Diesel's house so I can wait for him there, instead of walking me there? I don't want to take you away from your work."

Alice's expression darkened. In fact, if looks could kill, Juliana would have been smoked into a pile of ash where she stood.

Axel glanced in Alice's direction before giving Juliana a look that said he knew exactly what she was up to. He didn't seem upset about it, though.

"Nah. That's okay. I needed a break anyway." He pushed one of the swinging glass doors open for her and she exited, trying not to show the triumph in her face.

They walked along the sidewalk a few steps, then across the parking lot toward a large building called the Satellite Truck Wash. The scent of windshield washer fluid, soapsuds and damp air filled the air as they passed by.

Soon they came to a wide boardwalk lined with street lights. Juliana thought it would be nice for strolls in the dark. A wooden sign with a carved arrow said *Alienn, Arkansas only 500 steps away.* Someone had carved an additional message below the numbers that said, *More or less!*

"Is it really five hundred steps to Alienn?"

Axel laughed. "It is if you have a really long stride, maybe like a giraffe." He glanced down at her legs, assessing her stride length. "You might have to tack on a few more steps to *your* count, puny earthling."

"You all are really funny with that 'puny earthling' stuff," she said, picking up speed to match his steps.

"Well, we always aim to entertain our customers, so it comes naturally."

Juliana did her best to keep up with Axel's pace, which was healthy. The wooden boardwalk was weathered but well-built and in no time they were closer to the houses she'd noted in the distance when they started their 500-step journey.

"Is Alice an old girlfriend of Diesel's or something?"

He frowned. "No. Never. She's an employee. There are strict rules. Why?"

"She just seemed rather uncooperative from the first moment I stepped inside and asked for directions to Diesel's office. I'd never seen her before, but she seems to already have a dim view of me."

Axel pushed out a long sigh. "You have to understand this place is likely the biggest gossip mill in the state. When Diesel took off work on Friday—I'm assuming to go see you—rumors flew around like autumn wind driving piles of raked leaves into the swirling air."

"So what's the rumor?"

Axel shrugged, seemingly unwilling to share.

"Oh, come on. Tell me."

"The rumor I heard was that Diesel has a new secret girlfriend *out of town*." He stressed out of town like it was something gossip-worthy.

"Out of town? Meaning what?"

"Meaning not a girl from Alienn."

"He has to date someone from this town? That's a bit draconian and archaic, isn't it?"

"I didn't mean it like that. He can date anyone he wants, he just never has before. In fact, I don't know that he's ever even had a girlfriend."

"Why not?"

"Is this a trick question?"

"No. I'm just surprised. He's attractive and I've seen the way females talk to him and react to him."

Axel ran his hand though his hair in what seemed like a nervous gesture. "Listen, I'm not comfortable discussing his love life, but I will say he's very devoted to his job, likely because he took it over from our father last year."

"So he's never dated anyone? I find that hard to believe."

"He's dated. I think. Thing is, he's been busy with being the Fearless Leader up to now. Before he took over from our dad, he was in training for the job for years. Maybe now that he's settled in, he has more time for…distractions."

"Oh, is that what I am? A distraction?"

"I don't think he views you that way. Personally, I think it's a good thing."

"So what are the rumors about me?"

He hesitated, like he was afraid he might hurt her feelings. "It's not you in particular, but just that you're—well—an outsider."

"I see." But she *didn't* exactly get it. Anyone not from Alienn was an outsider? That didn't seem fair.

"Some folks are just suspicious of outsiders."

Juliana nodded. "Thank you for telling me."

"I didn't really tell you anything though, right?" He winked.

"That's right. You barely spoke on this walk over here. I simply have an intuition about such things." Juliana smiled at the thought of people gossiping about Diesel and his *outsider* girlfriend. However, she also considered the incident of the apple with the bite taken out of it that had so troubled Diesel.

"Do you know Alice very well?"

He shrugged. "I guess so. Why?"

"Would she be the kind of person to threaten someone?"

"Nah. I don't think so. It's not really like her."

"Are you sure?"

"What are you really asking?"

She debated about two seconds before spilling. "I found an apple on my doorstep with a single bite taken out of it. Diesel seemed rather upset about it. Actually, it happened twice. The first time was the day I met him and the second time was right before Diesel came to my apartment on Friday."

Axel's reaction was immediate. He stopped, grabbed her arm and stared into her eyes. "That's sort of a threat." He paused and looked all around the completely empty area where they stood.

"I know. Diesel told me. I find it interesting, but not threatening. He said it was a mild romance-related threat, but that he didn't have any other romance and he seemed to calm down."

"And you think Alice did it?" He looked back the way they'd come as if to ensure they weren't being followed.

"Well, she *was* a mean hag to me last night when I came into the store asking for Diesel. She interrupted us twice when we were about to kiss before we left."

Axel flashed a grin. "Is that so? Go, Diesel. I've never seen him so—" He paused as if he couldn't find quite the right word, finally settling on, "—

engaged with any woman. The truth is I don't keep up with any of my brothers' love lives. However, the few dates I ever saw Diesel on, he always seemed bored or like his thoughts were elsewhere. And that's *all* I'm willing to share."

"Interesting."

"Yeah. That's Diesel all right. He's interesting." He sounded distracted. He looked at the trail behind them again and said, "Come on. Let's get going."

"Why are you so troubled?"

"I'm not troubled. The info about the apple is just unexpected, that's all. Let's get you to Diesel's house, okay?"

Axel hustled her at a rapid pace to the end of the wooden boardwalk. They went down a couple of steps to cross several yards of grass and an empty space between two houses. Axel looked over his shoulder repeatedly.

They took a left when they reached the sidewalk, hurrying past three more houses along the tree-lined street. It was peaceful and warm and Juliana had a sudden desire to live here tucked away and gloriously happy.

Axel kept them moving at a brisk pace toward the end of the street. It wasn't a cul-de-sac, exactly, and didn't end with a circle and houses all around it. Instead, the street abruptly ended at a large two-story house with a wide porch running all the way across the front. It was blue with black shutters and had a dark cherry-red door. She loved it immediately and wanted to climb onto the very inviting porch swing and curl up with a good book.

"This is Diesel's place," Axel said. He guided her along the path in the lush green front yard that smelled recently mowed, headed for the porch.

"This is beautiful. I love it."

Axel tested the knob of the carved wooden front door. It opened right away. It hadn't been locked. Axel gestured for her to enter first. There was a light on in the hallway, but it wasn't needed. Probably Diesel had left it on for them last night, and they'd never gotten over here.

Instead, she'd been rather insistent they spend the night in his old room. He'd been easily convinced. Juliana had not a single regret, but she enjoyed seeing Diesel's home now.

She stepped across the threshold and onto hardwood floors set in a lovely two-story foyer. To her left was a charming wooden staircase leading straight up to the second floor, sporting a carpet runner in predominantly dark blue with some sort of pattern in the center.

To her right was an opening to the formal dining room with a lovely table and ten chairs. She could see another open doorway in the dining room, leading into a kitchen.

On her left, past the wall next to the staircase, was a living area with comfortable seating parked perfectly around a tall stone, wood-burning fireplace. Juliana breathed in the lingering scent of wood smoke in the air and smiled. She loved everything about a crackling fire, whether camping or simply in a fireplace, even when it was already warm enough.

Directly in front of her and to the right of the staircase was a straight shotgun hallway to a back door.

"It's older, but Diesel restored a lot of it himself over the past few years in what little spare time he enjoyed. What do you think?"

"Now that I'm inside, I love it more, especially since I know he worked to renovate it himself."

Axel closed and locked the front door, threw the deadbolt and put the chain in place right before testing the door handle as if to confirm it was secure.

"Should I be afraid that you just bolted us in here?"

"Um. No," he said unconvincingly, adding quickly, "Do you want something to drink? Or better yet, something to eat? I could probably rustle something up that's edible." He started down the hallway to the kitchen.

"No. I'm okay. I'll just wait for Diesel."

He motioned for her to follow him. "Well, I'll at least brew some coffee for us."

"You're staying?"

Axel stopped in his tracks. "I can't leave you alone."

"Why? Because of some fruit threat? Maybe I shouldn't have told you about that."

He opened his mouth to answer, but just then someone tried to open the front door, rattling the handle rather violently. Axel took a step toward the noise, but a buzzing sound stopped him. He plucked a small device off his belt. Before he even looked at it, whoever was at the door started rattling the handle again even harder. A large thump hit the door, like someone had thrown their shoulder against the outside surface trying to break it down. The heavy door practically shook in the doorframe from the abuse.

Axel ignored the buzzing and then subsequent ringing on his belt, marching toward the door. Juliana hoped it wasn't the fruit-wasting menace, chewing on the single bite they'd just taken out of an apple ready to hurl it at her once the door opened.

Axel put his hand on the door and then removed it. The pounding increased. He backed away another step, turned and glanced over his shoulder at her, a worried expression etched in his features.

"Are you going to answer it?" she asked, hoping he wasn't going to.

"I don't think I should."

Chapter 14

Diesel was fast losing his patience with this pretentious man from the Royal Caldera Cruise Line. "You already asked me that question, sir, and I answered. Twice." The quick fifteen-minute inspection tour he'd hoped for had already stretched to almost twice that time. Time he'd rather be spending with Juliana.

"Oh, yes. Indeed. Quite right, quite right." Inspector Centauri studied his electronic clipboard once more as if searching for more foolish questions to ask. The man had started repeating some of his questions a second and third time as if trying to see if Diesel was paying attention.

Diesel checked his watch about every ten seconds as the inspector asked him a rash of inane questions. Each and every one—while relevant to the business he wanted to engage in with this man—made his teeth ache because he wanted to be with Juliana, on their date, in his house, kissing.

"We've looked at every part of the truck stop that your guests would see unless they have special permission to tour outside the truck stop area and require a guide, which will be set up in advance or they won't go."

"Yes, yes. Understood. We might have an eccentric client every so often. However, the majority of our clientele would never consider this backwater planet for anything more than a quaint way station stop during their holiday. You don't have to worry about any exploration."

Diesel wasn't about to go out of his way to regale this pompous, arrogant man with information about how lovely Arkansas was or that this backwater planet had the tallest trees he'd ever seen. He also failed to share that each season had different temperatures and weather patterns that many Alphas who came here found charming and interesting. The inspector could suck it.

"Is that all, then? Do you have everything you need to complete your surprise inspection of our truck stop for future business here?"

They were in the northern basement section outside the area designated for travelers. It featured a variety of places to eat and lounge and rest as visitors watched human television, which many found fascinating as a pastime. There was also a wing filled with small rooms where clientele could sleep or rest in a quiet, private place away from the noise of the eating establishments.

"How many can you accommodate again?"

"Five hundred," Diesel said for the fourth time.

"Maybe you should write it down this time."

"Yes, yes. How long could we count on the services below stairs in cases of a scheduling delay or engine issues?"

Diesel opened his mouth to answer for the third time, but stopped. He crossed his arms and stared at the man. "Are you purposely trying to make this take longer than it needs to?"

"I beg your pardon?"

"You've seen everything. Some places twice. And your questions are starting to get repetitious. Meanwhile, I have somewhere else to be."

Inspector Centauri straightened and cleared his throat loudly. "Are you abandoning me?"

"Nope." Diesel pulled his communication device from his belt and texted Cam.

Come down to the north bunkers and relieve me from this arrogant ass of an inspector, or I can't be held responsible for my actions.

Cam sent a return text seconds later.

Be there in two minutes.

Now he was going to owe Cam a favor. Fine. It was worth it.

"What are you doing there?" Inspector Centauri asked.

"I'm getting another guide for you."

"You're the Fearless Leader. Isn't this *your* responsibility?'

"It is until I delegate it to someone else. You do

want to check out the security of our place, don't you?"

His head bobbled up and down. "Yes. Security is very important."

"I sent for the Security Officer. Besides, there's a safety issue involved." *It's your safety I'm worried about if I'm left alone with you much longer.*

"A safety issue?" The man looked around as if a gang of baddies was about to attack.

Cam showed up seconds later. "What's up?" He glanced at the stranger with obvious puzzlement.

"This is Inspector Centauri. He's doing a surprise inspection of our accommodations and services for the Royal Caldera Cruise Line, as per the way station contract Axel set up. I thought perhaps you'd like to show him that our security here surpasses none in this galaxy."

Cam brightened. "I'm happy to do that." Diesel knew Cam was very proud of the work he'd done to secure the underground and above-ground facilities.

"I'll send Axel to find you both later on."

Cam nodded absently, but his attention was on the inspector. "All right. Let's start with the below-ground security measures…" Cam went right into his spiel, talking as he walked Inspector Centauri away from Diesel.

Perfect. And not a moment too soon. He relaxed his fingers, letting go of the fists they were about to form.

Diesel hurried toward the exit that lead to the truck stop convenience store. He changed course for the rear exit, not wanting Alice or any of the other employees to stop him on his quest to get home and kiss Juliana.

As he came up the stairs, he saw Nova waiting for him, arms crossed, small slips of paper in her fingers and an expression that told him he needed to bear up for some news whether he liked it or not. "Whatever those little slips of paper say, they can wait until tomorrow. I have plans."

"There is someone here to see you. And your aunt Dixie is looking for you. I believe you should definitely talk to her."

"No, thanks. I don't want to talk to strangers and I especially don't want to talk to my aunt this moment. Any and all special projects she wants to enact are officially put on hold until tomorrow or, better yet, forever."

"Your aunt isn't going to like it."

"She never does."

"She's probably going to take your current neglect as permission to go through with her latest crazy plan if you don't take the time now to stop her."

"She's an adult." *In theory.* "She can do what she wants." *In theory.*

"There is also someone else here to see you, Diesel," Nova said. "I think you should talk to her." The tone in her voice was unrelenting.

"Who is here besides my aunt?"

"Says her name is Miss Penny."

Miss Penny? Diesel's brows furrowed. "A tiny, older woman that looks like a stiff wind gust would take her out?"

Nova frowned. "Yes. That describes her exactly. Do you know her?"

"We've met. Where is she?"

"I put her in your office."

Diesel went to see his unexpected visitor, but he was not happy about it. Stopping at his open office door, he saw Miss Penny seemingly mesmerized by the picture of a celestial, star-strewn rendering of his home galaxy, Caldera Forte.

The moment he opened the door wider, she shot away from the picture faster than he would have expected from someone as elderly and frail as she seemed to be. Perhaps she was not as delicate as she let on.

"Miss Penny? What brings you here tonight?"

She turned slowly to face him as if it pained her to do so. Her fragile smile was at war with the steely, unwavering gaze she sent his way. "I thought Juliana was here with you. She's really the one I need to speak to. Is she close by?" The old woman's gaze darted from the doorway back to his face with expectancy.

Diesel wondered how Miss Penny had arrived from almost an hour away when on Friday she'd needed Juliana's help to do her shopping, as well as what was so important to compel her to do so. "She's at my house—"

"Alone?!" Miss Penny stepped forward and her shriveled height seemed to grow astoundingly taller in the moment.

"My brother may still be with her." Diesel glanced at his watch. "Why? Is there a problem?"

Miss Penny seemed to realize the fragility she typically expressed was nowhere in sight. She inhaled deeply as if trying to calm herself.

"It's possible. But I truly need to ask her something."

"Must be important if you came all this way for a question," Diesel said. "Why don't you tell me what's really going on."

Miss Penny looked at him for a long while, her gaze uncertain, staring first at him and then drifting to the wall behind him before returning. She finally leaned forward and opened her mouth. Diesel thought she was going to confide in him. "Better not. Just take me to Juliana, please," she said with a polite smile.

Diesel grabbed his communicator and texted Axel.

Are you still at my house with Juliana?

He expected a quick response. Nothing came. He waited for a couple more beats, but still nothing. He changed the communicator for speaking and called him. No answer. He left a message. "Call me as soon as you get this."

"Take me to your home." Miss Penny said. "I'm afraid Juliana might be in trouble."

"Don't open the door," Juliana whispered urgently to Axel.

He turned, eyes squinting with curiosity. "Why? Do you know who's out there?"

"No. But what if it's, you know, a boogieman."

A half laugh, half grunt came from him. "A boogieman? Where'd you hear about that?"

"I'd rather not say."

"Well, trust me when I say the Boogieman doesn't knock," he said rather ominously. "Hold your horses!" Axel said loud enough for the outside knocker to hear, then added, "And stop pounding. I'm not opening this door!"

The pounding suddenly stopped. The abrupt silence was disquieting. Her ears rang from the previous loud banging. They both looked at the door. They looked at each other, shrugging as if recognizing it was truly strange.

Juliana wondered what had made the mad knocker stop. When they'd arrived, the door had been unlocked. Perhaps the pounder expected the door to be open and then become enraged when it wasn't. Maybe it was the apple menace ready to drop a barrel of half-eaten apples on the foyer floor.

Axel reached for the cell phone or whatever it

was on his belt. It looked like the one Diesel had.

"Who is it?"

"Diesel sent me a text asking if I was still here with you, then he called and left a message when I didn't pick up."

"Probably couldn't hear it over the pounding on the door."

He was pushing buttons on his phone when they heard car tires screech to a halt out front. Axel walked a few feet to a window facing the front yard and peeked out. She watched as his shoulders visibly dropped in relief.

"It's Diesel." He paused and added, "And he's not alone."

Juliana inhaled and exhaled, feeling better knowing Diesel was here. "He wasn't the one knocking, though, right?"

He shook his head. "No. He's racing up the sidewalk after leaping out of his truck, which is still running, I think. And he left the driver's door wide open, too. He's in a hurry."

Axel moved quickly to the front door to release the lock, the deadbolt and the chain. He popped the door open as Diesel took the porch stairs two at a time and practically launched himself through the door. He didn't stop moving until he grabbed Juliana into his warm embrace, buried his face against her neck and whispered, "I was worried about you."

Juliana wrapped her arms around him and

squeezed. "I was a little worried about me, too. Did you see who was outside?"

Diesel pulled back to stare into her eyes. Concern filled his gaze. "No. Who was outside?"

"I don't know, but they practically banged the door down pounding on it a few minutes ago."

Axel nodded. "Could have been an aggressive salesman, wanting to ensure they woke the dead to get someone to answer the door." He shrugged. "I was only spooked by what Juliana told me about finding an apple with a bite out of it tossed on her doorstep. Twice."

"Twice?!" Diesel shook his head and used a deliberately calm tone. "Not sure what that's about, but we can discuss it later. Okay?"

"Sure thing, bro." Axel grinned, like he looked forward to a discussion about someone tossing apples at her door.

Juliana noticed the elderly woman standing in the doorway looking rather confused. "Miss Penny," she said. She was shocked enough to release Diesel and move toward the front door. "What in the world are you doing here?"

Miss Penny's gaze darted around the entryway, looking more and more confused. Behind her, Juliana could see someone else approaching the house. The newcomer was also an elderly woman, but she didn't look confused. She looked madder than a hornet's nest beaten to the ground with a bat.

"Diesel Zebulon Grey!" she shouted from the yard as she approached the front door.

Axel and Diesel looked at each other and said at the exact same time, "Aunt Dixie."

"Who's Aunt Dixie?" Juliana asked.

Diesel walked toward the door. "She's our rather eccentric aunt."

"Diesel! I want to talk to you." The woman raced up the stairs to the door. The expression on her face seemed rather intense.

However, she slowed when she saw Juliana's neighbor on the doorstep. She put a hand on Miss Penny's shoulder, and said, "Hi. I'm Dixie Lou Grey. Want to join my women's group? It's a hoot."

Miss Penny's gaze hardened for a moment, which was very unlike her. Juliana wasn't certain why or even how Miss Penny had gotten herself to Alienn, Arkansas.

So Juliana was shocked when Miss Penny nodded. "Yes. I would like to be in a woman's group, especially if it's a hoot. What sorts of things do you all do in this women's group?"

Aunt Dixie threw her boney arms in the air with what looked like excitement. "Oh, lots of stuff. But mostly we think up ideas and fundraisers to benefit the Starlight Old Folks' Home on the outskirts of Alienn." She then pointed a thumb over her shoulder at Diesel. "Usually Our Fearless Leader, Mr. Spoilsport over there, shoots down every awesome idea we come up with. However, with some new blood in our ranks, maybe we'll finally be successful."

Juliana was shocked to her core when Miss Penny said, "Why, I'd love to join. Do I have to be a resident of the Starlight Old Folks' Home?"

"Course not. You don't even have to be a resident of Alienn. Besides, we can make you an honorary attendee, sort of like a...satellite member." She laughed as if that was the best joke ever told, elbowing Miss Penny in the arm. "Get it. A *satellite* member?" She laughed uproariously again and even slapped her knee.

Miss Penny smiled. "Yes. I get it. Because of your funny space-themed gas station. That's a good one."

"It's a truck stop," Diesel and Axel said.

"Whatever," Dixie said and wrapped an arm around Miss Penny's shoulders. "So, are you looking for residence in an old folks' home anytime soon? If you are, the Starlight is the best place on Earth to live for us old gals." The two elderly women turned away from the door and started ambling toward the yard, discussing the merits of living in an old folks' home versus living alone.

"I might be interested," Miss Penny said. "These old bones are getting mighty tired. And to tell the truth, I don't much like living by myself anymore."

"Miss Penny," Juliana said, her mouth still practically hanging open after finding her neighbor here at all. "What on earth are you doing in Alienn? How did you even get here?"

Diesel said, "Miss Penny needed to ask you an important question. Isn't that right, Miss Penny?"

Miss Penny looked over her shoulder at Juliana and the confused look returned. "I came looking for you, dear. I wanted to go get some groceries. You promised to take me. Did you forget again?"

"No. I didn't forget. I took you to get groceries on Friday. Don't *you* remember? And you didn't answer the question of how you got to Alienn."

Miss Penny gave an exaggerated eye roll to Diesel's Aunt Dixie and said, "Land sakes, child. It's no great mystery. I called Hail-A-Ride, and a nice young girl picked me up in her Subaru and brought me to the gas station...I mean, truck stop."

"You called Hail-A-Ride?" Juliana was living in an alternate reality.

"Yes. And it looks like I'll have to call them when I need to go get groceries from now on, since you're obviously too busy with your young man to take an old woman to the store."

Juliana pushed out a sigh, realizing she should be a better friend to her neighbor. "I'm sorry, Miss Penny. I didn't mean for you to travel all the way here to find me."

"Well, to be honest, I was also more than a little worried when you didn't come home last night." Miss Penny walked toward her a few steps and took one of Juliana's hands in hers. "No need to fret, though." She looked at Diesel, who had moved right behind her at the entryway of his home.

"Don't for a minute believe that I don't remember what it's like to be a young girl, free to go out with boys and believe you're falling in love. I remember all right and there's nothing wrong with it, to a point, Juliana." She frowned at Diesel. "Just make sure you don't give any milk away for free or else you might regret it, because why would a man buy a cow if he's already getting free milk."

"Miss Penny!" The heat of Juliana's embarrassment rippled from her belly to the top of her head. Her cheeks must be the color of a fire engine. How did Miss Penny even guess what had happened the night before? Was she psychic all of a sudden as well as being befuddled when it came to grocery shopping?

Aunt Dixie marched up to the front door to rejoin the group. She poked Diesel in the chest with her forefinger and asked, "Have you already gotten free milk, Diesel? If so, it seems like you should go ahead and buy the cow. Don't you think that's the right thing to do in this situation?"

Chapter 15

Diesel couldn't speak for a moment, finding himself in one of the most horrifyingly uncomfortable situations of his life. And that was saying a lot, considering he'd faced down a malevolent being racing through town unchecked not too long ago, but the current free milk-and-cow discussion certainly surpassed that on the fear scale by an exponential factor. He absolutely did not want to discuss his love life with his crazy aunt or Juliana's confused, nosy neighbor in a public place, or ever, really.

His aunt crossed her arms, impatiently tapping one foot on the porch as she waited for him to answer the question of whether he was going to buy a cow if he'd already gotten free milk, which every person standing here knew meant they wanted to know if he and Juliana had slept together.

It was no one else's business, and time to end this ridiculous confrontation.

Behind him, Axel poked him in the shoulder

and said in a low tone, "Bro, I'm totally on your side here, but you should really consider buying the cow. It's the right thing to do. My two cents."

Juliana gave Axel an incredulous look.

Diesel said in an equally low tone, "You're not helping."

Axel grinned. "Well, what *can* I do to help?"

Diesel pointed to his truck and said, "My keys are still in the ignition. Take Aunt Dixie back to the truck stop and help Juliana's neighbor get back home to Doraydo, with more groceries if she needs them. *That* would be a big help."

"Will do. And I won't even expect a response to the free milk-and-cow questions that have gone unanswered, but don't think I didn't notice."

"Whatever," Diesel said under his breath. He made an announcement to the group. "Listen up. Axel is in charge of taking care of the two of you." He pointed to both Miss Penny and Aunt Dixie. "Do what he says, or else."

"Or else what?" Dixie said, her gaze narrowing suspiciously.

"Or else he'll take away the all-you-can-eat-anytime-of-day-Jell-O policy at the Starlight Old Folks' Home," Axel said, winking at Diesel over one shoulder.

"He wouldn't dare. That's blasphemy." Dixie uncrossed her arms to plant them firmly on her hips.

Axel stepped out onto the porch. "If you start talking about cows and free milk again he might, so let's go, ladies." Axel somehow managed to herd the two elderly women toward Diesel's truck, loading them into the front seat before driving away.

"I don't understand why Miss Penny came all the way here."

Diesel squinted in the direction of the departing truck. "She said she was worried about you. Maybe she realized you didn't come home last night and wanted to ensure you understood the whole free milk-and-cow theory she wanted to impart."

"Yeah, about that—"

"You're about to ask me if I want me to buy a cow, aren't you?" Diesel didn't have mixed feelings about Juliana. He wanted her. He expected her to be in his life from now on. There were hurdles, of course, but he wasn't ready to discuss them yet. He'd marry her today if she knew he was an alien from another planet. However, it was too early to explain his true heritage and that to be together they'd possibly have to move to another galaxy.

"No. I don't have a cow. You aren't telling me that I *am* a cow, right?"

"That's exactly right. You are not a cow and besides I don't want to buy any livestock."

Before she could respond, the grandfather clock in the hallway started chiming the tenth hour.

"Listen, why don't we forget about elderly women trying to get into our business? Because it isn't their business.

"Instead, we'll spend the day together visiting

wherever you want in town. I can even see if the mayor will let us inside the courthouse to look at the picture of Bonnie and Clyde at the speakeasy for your article."

"Okay. That sounds perfect, and if I *never* hear the words 'free milk' or 'cow' again in the same sentence, I'll be deliriously happy."

He raised his left hand. "I solemnly swear you won't hear them from me."

"Good." Juliana also looked at the departing truck. "Are we going to walk around town?"

"We can, but I have another vehicle, sort of, if you want to take a look." He grinned at her. "It's fun, too."

A smile shaped her lips. "What is it?"

Diesel led her to the garage, which was attached to the back of the house by a short screened-in walkway. He opened the door and led her inside a large three-car space. He pushed a button on the wall and the far door started to lift. The bright morning sun revealed a large red four-wheeler in the third stall.

"Is that even street legal?" she asked with a laugh.

"Are you kidding? In Arkansas? Does a bear," he paused only slightly and finished with, "*poop* in the woods?"

She laughed. "My answer to that is yes, and also I'd love to ride your obviously street legal Arkansas four-wheeler all through town."

"Then let's ride." He grabbed a set of keys off a hook by the door and they passed two empty stalls to reach his "fun" vehicle.

Snuggled up behind Diesel on a loud four-wheeler racing through Alienn was exactly how she enjoyed the rest of her day. The few townspeople they saw seemed surprised, but Diesel didn't slow down or talk to anyone but her. He even gave them safety helmets wired with speakers and mics so they could talk and still hear over the throttle, going full blast, during the entire fun ride.

After crisscrossing several the streets in downtown Alienn where he pointed out various interesting town facts, Diesel then took her to the former bank with the basement speakeasy. They parked and he took her on a tour. There was not much left to see but a big empty building sporting a few broken pieces of glass and a dusty, dank space filled with cobwebs and dust. Still, Juliana reveled in spending the day with Diesel.

Diesel somehow convinced the mayor to open the courthouse for a special private visit. They toured the mini museum housed within the courthouse where the Bonnie and Clyde picture was on display behind glass, reading the bit of documentation available as to theories on what had happened back in the day.

Juliana also saw an old picture of Alienne Greenly, the founder of Alienn, Arkansas, a diorama of the Bauxite mine as it was back in 1963, and a picture of an empty mining town in the northwest, along with the legend and speculation of what happened to some former lost colony that all disappeared without a trace over 150 years ago.

Diesel pointed out other interesting things in the museum before they left and she even got a souvenir, replica copy of Bonnie and Clyde's picture in the old speakeasy.

They talked about everything—their pasts, their present and what they wanted for their futures. He mentioned the "tradition" of dating locally, but that it wasn't carved in stone. He didn't dwell on it or make it seem like he was worried about it. He also didn't mention the issue of someone throwing apples at her doorstep at all, for which she was grateful. She'd just as soon forget all about any threat.

Juliana wanted to only spend her time with this incredible man from now on. The article she needed to write practically wrote itself in her mind from the notes she'd taken at the speakeasy and the courthouse. Before the day ended, she could honestly say she was falling in love with Diesel. He was perfect. He made her heart swell with joy each moment they spent together.

Diesel was the one. Her one. She knew it. He'd even volunteered to go with her in search of her past because he didn't want to miss a day with her. No one in her life had ever made her feel as special as Diesel did in a single weekend together.

Once back at his house, he gave her another nickel tour, but insisted on making her dinner before showing her the master bedroom, which she found very romantic.

He further romanced her, cooking a dinner that included ham steaks, baked potatoes, green beans and cornbread with honey butter that was so rich and tasty it could have served as dessert. And all of it was accompanied by strong sweet tea, a southern staple of many evening meals.

After supper they took their iced tea to the screened-in back porch, taking in the view as they sat together holding hands until dark, talking about everything and nothing.

Once they retired inside, and put their glasses in the sink, Diesel grabbed her close and kissed her like he never wanted their lip lock to end. She certainly didn't intend to stop.

He danced her through the kitchen and down the hallway to his master bedroom, the one he didn't show her until now. Opening the door, he broke the kiss long enough to usher her inside and close the door behind him.

Diesel's master bedroom was beautiful. Simple, and yet the wood furniture and massive bed were all very inviting in a comfortable style. This was exactly where she wanted to spend the night.

Earlier, they'd taken the four-wheeler back to the Big Bang Truck Stop so she could retrieve her car. In the trunk she had that small overnight bag she'd packed, which she left on his living room sofa during the initial tour.

Diesel kissed her again, dancing her toward his large bed. He kissed her cheeks, he kissed her chin. He trailed kisses from her jawline to the tickly place on her neck right beneath her ear. He knew she liked being kissed there from the last time they'd been in a bedroom together.

She was lost to his intimate attention. She never wanted to leave his warm company. Juliana expected it would be another completely magical evening.

By morning's first light, she was proven correct. The previous evening together had been even more magical than the first.

Spending the night in Diesel's home had been fairy-tale-like all the way down to having a charming prince keeping her up most of the night. But that was perfectly fine. Her only disappointment was when he had to leave early to go to work, as it was Monday. He expected a very busy coming week at the truck stop and told her not to freak out if he wasn't able to call or talk to her for the next few days.

The night before she'd told him she had to head home and spend the week writing her article, as the submission date was fast approaching. He kissed her forehead, told her he'd do his best to call her before the end of the week to check up on her, and left her sleepy and dozing.

Juliana slid out of Diesel's bed a couple of hours later, found the coffee pot he'd left on warm for her and downed two cups to wake up. She fetched her overnight bag from the sofa, showered in his massive bathroom and then strolled around his house looking at various things that made her delighted to be in his company.

She was upstairs when she was startled by the sound of a loud noise from somewhere on the lower floor. It sounded liked a door slamming. Had Diesel come back? Juliana went downstairs and carefully and quietly explored the lower floor, calling his name and desperately hoping no one jumped out at her. She'd probably drop into a dead faint if she saw a boogieman. Whatever they looked like.

She noticed the door to his home office was ajar. Hadn't Diesel closed it last night? She'd only poked her head inside for a quick glance during his nickel tour. He hadn't wanted her to look too closely, telling her it was sort of a mess. She'd seen a desk strewn with paper and not much else.

Juliana pushed the door open wider and hoped again that no one would jump out at her, but wanting to check every room to ensure no one lingered waiting to get her.

She noticed a picture of Maxwell the Martian on the wall behind his desk and smiled, not only because she found it endearing, but also because the frame wasn't straight.

Juliana walked over to the wall intent on leveling the frame. As soon as she twisted the frame back into place, an invisible door appeared in the otherwise empty wall, opening into a hidden space about the same size as his office.

Awesome. A secret door.

Maybe this was why he hadn't wanted her to see the room too closely. Last night, he'd said he hadn't spent much time in his office lately, but mostly it was a mess.

She hesitated only briefly before stepping inside the hidden room. The lights in the ceiling came on automatically. She saw several outer space pictures on the wall. Along one low shelf were eight-by-ten picture frames showing Diesel and what looked like his large family in a barren and alien-looking environment. Arizona, maybe?

She recognized Cam and Axel in a candid group photo. The others in the family photo certainly looked related. The caption on the frame read, "Family trip, Alpha-Prime," with a date from a few years ago.

What? Alpha-Prime? That sounded very familiar. Where had she heard that name before?

Wasn't that what the strange man in the even stranger suit had said? That his coat was made with standard Alpha-Prime material or something like that. She'd been sleepy and had totally forgotten about it during the rest of her Sunday with Diesel.

She turned to the desk, not wanting to snoop, exactly, but hoping to understand the growing suspicion that perhaps aliens did run loose here, living in plain sight. Could it be true? Really true?

The memory of the creature she'd seen in her dream rose in her mind with even more specific detail. Diesel, hand lovingly on her back, had led her out the employee door. And they'd seen the creature about to enter what looked like a basement bomb shelter. Odd, since basements of any kind were rare in this part of the country. An Arkansas basement was an invitation for flooding or at the very least water seepage on a regular basis.

Next, his brother Cam had raced onto the shocking scene. He'd pointed a small bullhorn at Juliana and she'd woken up in her car with a lack of memories.

Juliana felt a wave of dizziness hit her, hard. She sat down at the messy, paper-strewn desk as memories of going back into the convenience store for a second time and starting the conversation with Diesel all over again filled in a more realistic timeline. She hadn't been asleep. Her memories had been erased and she'd gone back inside a second time.

Juliana remembered both times she'd met Diesel. But the second time, Diesel pretended not to remember the first time they'd met. Why would he do that? Why would he pretend they didn't know each other? That they hadn't kissed that first glorious time?

She closed her eyes and remembered clearly kissing him for the very first time. Magical—just like sleeping with him—was the best word to describe the experience. She'd asked a question he didn't want to answer. He'd been trying to kiss her to distraction. It had worked, sort of.

Elbows on the surface of this desk, head resting on her fists, Juliana allowed the dream-like memories to repopulate in her mind, staring at the surface of this cluttered desk, but not really seeing what was there.

At least not at first. Her mind started working to fill in the blanks. As the dream-like memories coalesced, she registered what was on Diesel's secret desk, in his secret office, filled with a multitude of secret odd pictures showcasing him and his family in secret odd places, or rather secret places not of this world.

The papers on his desk were varying colors, but primarily gray. Many had a heading that indicated they were from the Alpha-Prime place. She studied a few documents on top of one pile, but didn't recognize the language. In fact, whatever this was it didn't look like anything she'd ever seen before.

Juliana's college degree was in communication. On her own time, she'd studied several languages enough to identify them, though not well enough to speak them. The letters, words and symbols on these pages were something she'd never seen before. They were strange, unidentifiable and even holographic in some places. Definitely alien.

There were also several more pictures with the words Alpha-Prime written in the description. One showed what looked to be an alien spacecraft getting ready to depart into space. It looked like something out of a science-fiction movie.

A small stack of white paper caught her eye, since it was handwritten in English and looked like a personal letter. She picked it up from the center of the blotter and saw that there were actually three letters. It was as if Diesel had opened them, scanned through them and dropped them in a pile as if they held no further significance.

Or perhaps the stack had been left there because he hadn't finished reading it, perhaps planning to look at it later. She might have ignored it further, only noticing it at all because she saw Diesel's name at the top in an intimate greeting. Her heart almost seized in her chest.

The first letter was dated three months ago and began:

My darling, wonderful Diesel,

Juliana picked the letter up and read the whole thing. Twice. She then folded her arms in front of her, dropped her head down and cried her eyes out.

The second letter opened with, *Dear Diesel,* and contained a confused-sounding single-page message that wondered why the writer hadn't heard anything from him. It was signed, *still madly in love with you, but please contact me.*

The third letter was dated last month. It was terse and angry.

Diesel,

It's clear you never intended to fall madly in love with me. Nor did you obviously ever care for me. I've left message after message, and you've ignored every one of them. No one is this busy. Therefore, I can only assume that you lied to me about every single thing you said. I'm not special. You only took what you wanted and threw me aside. You're a vile, reprehensible person, and also I'm not *madly in love with you anymore.*

Adele

Once Juliana finished reading all three letters and her impromptu crying jag, she stood up and walked around the desk, deciding to take a closer look at the memorabilia placed in the secret office. She noticed what looked like an old-fashioned photo album, filled with page after page of illuminating pictures.

She thumbed through it until she found a picture of the half octopus-half man she'd dreamed about. On the back it said Resident of Moogally. Whatever that was. She slipped it out of the sleeve and put it in her purse along with a picture of Diesel with his family and the handwritten caption, "Away from Earth, vacationing on Alpha-Prime."

She should be elated she'd found a treasure trove of possible facts that pointed to the notion aliens from another planet did indeed live and work in plain sight. She should be elated she had something to write for her coming article. Unfortunately, it came at the cost of her heart.

After spending this intimate weekend with Diesel, she'd been about to write some idiot fiction piece about a pair of infamous bank robbers from early in the last century who *may* have robbed the Alienn Bank, but her broken heart wouldn't let her forget the letters on the desk from a recent, apparently short-lived relationship Diesel shared with someone who'd signed the letter, "Madly in love with you, too. Always and forever, Adele." That woman had summarily gotten her heart stomped on when Diesel apparently had gotten all he wanted from the poor girl and ditched her. Was that about to be Juliana's fate?

Juliana read the first love letter from Adele again as more tears streamed down her face. All the supposedly special and magical things they'd done together—the fortune from Maxwell the Martian saying, "Our Fearless Leader thinks you're pretty, too"; the ride through town on his four-wheeler;

spending that first night at his parents' house—were noted in the letter.

No special moment was left out. The mugs of coffee drank while seated at his parents' kitchen island were referenced. He'd made this Adele person pancakes the next morning, too. The special ham dinner with sweet yummy cornbread had all been used on another girl, a human girl, just like herself.

According to the letter, Adele had come to the truck stop asking if there were really aliens in Alienn, Arkansas, and Diesel had promptly swung into action. He'd deflected the truth about aliens living in Alienn in the exact same way he had with Juliana, all the way down to telling her he'd be busy for the next few days when the sexy weekend was over, but that he'd call her.

But he hadn't called Adele, or taken her calls, or called her back or remembered she existed at all after he got what he wanted, also according to subsequent letters months later.

Adele had apparently been trying to get hold of him for quite a while, if the dates on the letters were any indication, gushing about how she had fallen madly in love with him. Mentioning how romantic it had been that after only knowing each other a short time, he planned to fall madly in love with her.

That was the single most hurtful sentence in the entire set of letters.

The line she'd thought was so very romantic when he said it to her in his office. Juliana had believed all of the other things he'd said to her and done with her had been special and unique to their day together.

However, Adele's first letter detailed many of the exact same special things that she and Diesel had *also* done together.

These must have all been simply his typical moves in order to sleep with human girls and keep them from believing there were aliens roaming around here. Adele had been duped. Juliana had been duped. She'd been so amazingly foolish.

Juliana shook off the hurt and the humiliation and leapt into action. She grabbed her bag, headed to her car, and drove straight back to Doraydo. She'd been a complete fool to expect a gorgeous man—or gorgeous alien—like Diesel would ever be interested in a nobody like her.

She needed to get home on familiar turf, think through everything and then make a plan for what she'd do next.

Diesel didn't have to worry about giving her the brush off or about ever seeing her again. She wouldn't look for a call from him and she also wouldn't bother writing him any heartfelt lovelorn letters like Adele had, beseeching him to come back or even to call and explain.

Apparently, once he was done with a girl, he

never called or saw her again. That was just fine. It would make it much easier.

Juliana was done. She'd write her article and let the chips—or rather her astonishing discovery of aliens living on planet Earth—fall where they may.

Chapter 16

Friday morning

Diesel had been so busy with all the crazy things going on in the basement complex, he hadn't realized so many days had gone by since he'd left Juliana warm in his bed. It was Friday, but he hadn't been home all week, sleeping instead in the quarters provided to spacecraft passengers.

He hadn't heard from Juliana all week, and he likely wouldn't have had time to even say hello even if she'd called. He'd have to check with Nova and see if Juliana had left any messages that hadn't filtered downstairs to him just yet. He'd tried to warn her his week was going to be busy, but even he hadn't realized what was in store for him. His Monday had started out with his brothers Jack and Wheeler. He'd set them on a secret project to possibly thwart a problem he wasn't certain he'd ever have, but better safe than sorry.

They were almost finished talking when he was notified the first flight on the addendum of the new contract had crashed in the woods near a small Georgia town he'd never heard of called Nocturne Falls. From that point, it had been all hands on deck all week long.

Diesel had sent a team, of course, with a mission to hide the craft and recover the three people aboard the ill-fated flight. Stella Grey, Elise Greene and Victoria Midori, his very best crew, had gone out shortly after the report came in.

Cam had shouldered the heaviest part of the load after the initial team had been sent, because he was in security. Axel was typically in charge of the communications regarding recovery, but much still had to be done to ensure no humans found out about it, so Diesel was helping out where he could.

To that end, he'd spent hours and hours scanning for any tidbits of information on the human airwaves and Internet that might have signaled the cloaking device hadn't worked as intended when the small craft crashed. Axel had also been very involved, since he'd set up the whole addendum and primary contract flight for extra money in the first place.

Luckily, it didn't seem any earthlings had discovered or even suspected that a UFO had crashed. However, of the three people aboard, one had been a prisoner. The other two were the guard and the pilot. They were also missing.

Another express ship had been sent from Alpha-Prime to retrieve the prisoner bound for Galactic

Gulag XkR-9 and get him there as soon as possible.

Diesel had lots of balls in the air and he was glad he'd told Juliana he'd be busy for the next few days. But he missed her terribly. In the rare extra seconds he'd had over the last several days, he'd thought about her, wanting to wrap her in his embrace, rest his cheek on the top of her head and simply hold her close.

Alas, that was not to be, at least not in the near future, but hopefully soon. After five days without contact or even hearing her voice, he needed to call her and touch base. Luckily, he'd had the wherewithal to send flowers to her home the morning she'd returned, right after learning of the UFO crash, knowing he'd be busy for the next several days.

In the few spare minutes between important chores, he'd contemplated whether he'd have to give up his career. His choices were simple. In fact, there were only two.

The first was to keep her in the dark forever and always about the alien presence on Earth, which also meant a regular Defender blast to ensure she had no knowledge. He didn't like that option.

The second option involved convincing her to move to Alpha-Prime with him and start over there once she learned he was an alien from outer space. While he wasn't opposed to that in order to spend the rest of his life with Juliana, his true love, he did wish there was a better option to staying on Earth than blasting her with a Defender when she learned about something alien or Alpha-Prime related. It also might be more frequent than he'd be comfortable with on a day to day basis.

With their parents and sister still out of town, Cam had wanted to continue the check of the houses. His brother had mentioned in passing this morning that when he'd had one of his people check their parents' home he'd also had someone check Diesel's house, since he'd allowed the human to stay there unattended and hadn't been back all week.

Diesel had blurted out a vulgar two-word phase in his head. He realized his brother was as stressed as he was about the whole issue with the downed spacecraft in an out-of-state location and also out of their immediate control.

Instead of a curse, the two words he said out loud were, "Thank you."

Cam must have heard the attitude in his tone, though, because he added, "My employee said your back door was left unlocked, by the way. You're lucky no one got in there and stole everything you own."

Diesel had checked all the doors before he left Juliana there. He'd wanted to ensure she was safe. "I checked the back door that morning before I left. It was locked."

"Maybe *your earthling* forgot and left it unlocked when she went off to her home in Doraydo."

"Maybe," Diesel said, but they'd talked about it the night before. He'd been concerned about the still unknown apple-throwing menace. "And her name is Juliana, not *'your earthling,'* by the way."

Cam huffed, but didn't otherwise respond.

Diesel was surprised to learn his back door had been left unlocked, but it was understandable. However, when Axel had accompanied Juliana to his home last Sunday, he mentioned finding his front door unlocked before someone had tried the handle and then practically broken the door down.

He would have sworn he'd locked his house up before leaving Saturday morning. Then again, his mind had been filled with the possibilities of not only Juliana's first visit to his home, but also showing her his life and seriously contemplating a future together.

There were a few things to consider on both sides of the equation.

Diesel was calmer and happier in her company than he'd ever been with any other. Spending the night with her in his old room had been wildly unexpected, but he'd known she was the one for him. He'd known she was the only one he'd ever want. If Juliana wasn't going to be in his life, then he'd rather live alone and die as soon as possible to end his grief.

During a rare break, Diesel went upstairs to his office and called Juliana. He just needed to hear her voice. Unfortunately, he only got her voicemail, but at least he got to hear her ask him to leave a message. He relaxed just hearing the recording. How foolish was that?

"Hi, Juliana. I'm sorry I haven't had a chance to call you until now. It's been rather busy at work. Hopefully you got the flowers I sent and I meant every word on the note." He smiled to himself. In the note, he told her his plan to fall madly in love with her seemed to be progressing very well and he expected to fall in love with her any second.

He relished every moment they'd spent together, whether on his four-wheeler riding through town or getting a fortune from Maxwell the Martian.

"I'm hoping to have some free time this weekend and I wondered when we could see each other. I miss you terribly. Please call and leave a message, if you'd like." He wanted to tell her he loved her. Was it too soon? "My plan to fall madly in love with you is working perfectly. I love you and also I miss you rather desperately."

Diesel was goofy over and completely in love with an earthling. The urge to laugh like a loon rose up, but he tamped it down. He needed to focus on his current problems and simply look forward to his future with Juliana when time allowed.

Diesel hung up and scrubbed his hands over his face. He needed to get back downstairs and finish his search of the human airwaves. But he wanted to wait and see if Juliana got his message in the next few minutes and called him back.

Was he a sap, sitting here waiting for a girl to call him? Maybe he was a lovesick, foolish idiot, but he'd already declared to her his plan had worked.

If Juliana didn't return his feelings of love—surely a ridiculous notion—Diesel would live the rest of his life miserable and alone.

No one else anywhere in this galaxy or the next would do.

Very early Friday morning

Juliana had spent the last several days writing the article for Finder's. In fact, she'd written two articles. The two versions were vastly different in subject, tone and revelations regarding aliens living on planet Earth. The first draft included her conviction that there were aliens living in southern Arkansas, hiding in plain sight at a famous truck stop on Route 88. She detailed her experiences from her first visit to her last, when she'd acquired the photographic evidence.

When she wasn't butt in chair, fingers on keyboard working on her article, she was pacing the floor angry with herself for the endless tears she'd shed after leaving Alienn and Diesel on Monday.

She told herself he'd call or send a note or maybe even flowers, but nothing had come. Zero. Zip. Zilch. There had not been a single attempt to communicate in any way.

It was more difficult than she thought to hold on to the anger she'd felt while reading Adele's letter. It was heartbreaking to learn that all the things he'd done to make her fall in love with him were not special at all. He'd used the same lines, the same date and the same everything to basically get her into bed. Well, to make her want him and love him anyway.

But then she'd remember that *she* was the one who'd insisted on staying overnight in his room. Or had he cleverly played on her vulnerable feelings?

Had he used his wily alien mind control on her to make her think spending the night with him had been her own idea? No. Well, maybe. She wasn't sure anymore. Each day away from him lessened her ire. Each day away from him made her exceedingly lonely, as if the physical distance from him caused her melancholy, which was crazy.

There hadn't been any more apples thrown at her doorstep, making her wonder if the mysterious Adele of the letters had even been responsible in the first place.

Until finding the secret room behind the fake wall in Diesel's home office, Juliana had been certain he was the only man for her. She'd even contemplated not using the money from this article to fund a trip to the northwest, instead perhaps spending it on a wedding dress.

At least until she read Adele's letters. The crushing, heart-rending messages she'd found had absolutely changed everything. Realizing that aliens lived among earthlings in Arkansas should have been another earth-shattering discovery, but in her current emotional state, it only rated second place in the *shock and awe* category of her love life.

By mid-week she wished she was blissfully ignorant of those stupid letters. She should never have sneaked into his hidden office. Or stolen pictures of his alien world to write a story filled with innuendo about aliens among them. She didn't have the best proof. Any picture could be doctored. But in her heart of hearts and deep in her soul, she knew it was true.

The memories she recalled had helped and the conversations Diesel and his brother shared while she was unconscious had nonetheless filtered into her brain. It was like she'd only been playing possum after being shot with the megaphone, or what they'd called the Defender. She found she remembered quite a lot of her missing time in Alienn, especially at the truck stop.

He greeted you like it was the first time he'd ever met you, twice. Whatever else he was, Diesel was an excellent actor when called for.

Last night she'd weakened and quickly wrote

the article about Alienn that didn't out them all for being from another planet, or living in secret for some reason that wasn't clear.

Instead, she used the story Diesel told her about the infamous couple who had stopped in at a speakeasy and possibly robbed the bank in Alienn, even though there was no official proof of that. Still, why waste the notes?

Pacing back and forth behind her sofa, Juliana thought about her two very different stories. Each would be a good submission to the special Finder's book.

Tomorrow morning was Friday—given the late hour, technically it was already Friday—and her article was due. She'd have to personally deliver it to Mr. Harriman so he could review it and make his decision on whether she made the cut for the special book.

Which one should she submit?

She didn't need to be rushed right now. Mr. Harriman had not really apologized for the change in deadline when they'd spoken on Monday, only told her that due to some special publicity, all the articles being considered for inclusion had to be turned in early. Instead of two more weeks, he needed her piece by Friday morning at the latest and she must deliver it in person so she could sign the release.

Was she truly going to reveal her suspicions about aliens living on Earth? She plopped down on her sofa to think about the ramifications of both articles. She needed to ponder the pros and cons.

If she went with the one that outed Diesel and his family, they probably wouldn't like it. Would she start a war of the worlds between Earth and Alpha-Prime? Would Diesel track her down and recreate the Boogieman Affair when he found out she'd tattled? Would he throw bushels of apples at her with a single bite taken out of each one? Did she really just want to see Diesel again?

Deep down in her soul, the real answer was a resounding, "Yes!" Obviously she was conflicted.

If she went with the initial story she'd planned—the one he'd likely fabricated for her—about the infamous Bonnie and Clyde drinking in the local speakeasy and possibly robbing a bank in Alienn, she might never have to see him ever again. Would that be for the best? Probably.

The article implying aliens lived among them would certainly get a response and Diesel might come knocking on her door. What would he say? Would he try to romance her and get her to recant the story? Would he kiss her every time she asked a question he didn't want to answer? A smile shaped her lips before she could stop it.

In the article about the bank robbers, she mentioned aliens as a quaint local legend, but ultimately dismissed the notion as farfetched.

Either way she could take the money from the article and head back to Washington State to learn what she could about her own history. She'd be all alone, not traveling with Diesel holding her hand the whole time because he simply couldn't live without her. That wasn't even true. He hadn't called all week and she shouldn't expect he would.

After she got back on Monday, she'd been writing when she thought she heard voices outside her door. When she finally got up to look, no one was there.

She sniffed the tears away and then sniffed some more, curling into a ball on the sofa and dozed off without making any decisions. Juliana dreamed of Diesel and the time they'd spent together. She wished her broken heart wasn't as vocal and disparaging as her forgiving soul was with regard to this situation.

Juliana heard a phone ringing in her dream, but couldn't find it. When her dream-self went to answer it, Diesel's brother Cam was there with a cannon-sized megaphone ready to zap her until she forgot everything forever.

What is ringing?

She opened her eyes and sat up on the sofa. Sunshine was now streaming in through the living room window into her face. She must have fallen asleep trying to decide which article to turn in. *What time is it?*

Juliana glanced up at the clock and realized she had leave her apartment in less than ten minutes to get to Mr. Harriman's office on time or forfeit the incredible offer and the money that went with it.

She spent four minutes in the shower, three minutes brushing her teeth and combing her hair into a loose, messy, damp ponytail, two minutes putting fresh clothes on even though she wasn't completely dry from her speedy shower and was ready to leave her place with less than a minute to spare.

She hustled out to the living room, grabbed her purse and looked down at both articles on the table behind the sofa. She put her hand on one and read the first line. Moving her fingertips to rest on the other, she read that first line. She wavered about which she should choose. The flashing message light on her home phone caught her eye and she saw it was time to go right now.

Juliana pushed out a long breath and made her final decision. She picked one article up and flew out the door, knowing that if she spent one second longer deciding, she'd be too late to turn in either story.

Chapter 17

Diesel was tired all the way to his marrow when he stepped inside his home Friday afternoon. The last time he'd been here, he'd kissed a sleep-rumpled Juliana goodbye and headed to work after the most amazing time off he'd ever spent. He was madly in love with an earthling. He couldn't wait to see Juliana again, hold her in his arms, and especially kiss her silly.

Walking through his home to head upstairs, he saw his open home office door and paused. He always kept it closed. Now, it was ajar. He'd popped it open briefly when showing Juliana his home, but remembered distinctly closing the door until the latch clicked. There was no use tempting fate by allowing her close to his alien artifact-laden hidden room.

Had Juliana gone into his office? A panicked feeling dove deeply into his belly at the idea she'd found his hidden space, though he knew it was highly unlikely. He walked slowly to the door and looked in. The room appeared to be fine. Maxwell's picture was perfectly straight and nothing seemed out of place. He pushed out a sigh of relief and closed the door, ensuring it latched this time.

Diesel went upstairs to clean up, intending to head straight to Juliana's place in Doraydo. He needed to see her, needed to hug her tight, kiss her gently and hold her in his embrace until she understood what being madly in love meant to him.

She was very important to his future happiness. He might have to accept some rather large sacrifices in order to make her his bride, but he was ready to do it. He would hand over his career on Earth and go back to Alpha-Prime so they could be together forever, if that was his only option. He just hoped she was open-minded about space travel.

An hour later he was standing in front of Juliana's door with flowers. He knocked hard, wanting to get her attention. Her front door popped wide open of its own volition. A thin line of panic streaked down his spine. "Juliana!" he called through the widening space. "Your door is open." No response.

Diesel stepped across the threshold, closing the door behind him. He walked down the hallway to her bedroom. Her bed was made. The light was still on in the bathroom and girly stuff was scattered on the counter as if she'd gotten ready and left in a big hurry. He shut the light off and exited her bathroom. He stared at her undisturbed

bed, feeling like something was off, but unable to see what. He left her bedroom, walking down the hallway until he stood behind the sofa. He wondered if she'd be upset if he waited for her.

Looking down, he noticed a stack of papers on the table. He read the title, *You've Got Aliens*, and smiled at the cleverness. He scanned down to read the first line and his entire body froze. *Aliens do exist right in plain sight at the Big Bang Truck Stop in Alienn, Arkansas on Route 88 and I can prove it!* Diesel picked the article up and read the entire thing.

It was clear from the article that not only had she found his secret office, she'd taken some of his personal pictures from there before leaving, including one that looked like a half octopus-half man alien that she'd personally witnessed.

Her tone throughout the entire story was hostile, angry and mean. The article was meant to enflame and incite anyone reading it. The Finder's book people would probably love it.

She even mentioned the Defender with a warning to watch out, as it made memories seem like dreams, which was a big problem because how did she know the name of something that was supposed to have completely erased her mind for a defined time period? She had a few memories, but she'd written about things she could have only heard while she was unconscious. So she remembered everything and realized it wasn't a dream.

If this article was published in a Finder's special edition book, folks from all over the country would come to discover if aliens from Alpha-Prime had been fooling humans for decades. Diesel was in big trouble if this was the article she'd written for publication.

He took minor solace in the fact Finder's wouldn't simply take her word for it on a story this big. They'd send someone to verify her wild, crazy claims, which weren't wild or crazy, but quite factual.

If the Finder's representative garnered even a hint of truth in what she'd written, the publication would likely go with it. And if she gave them some pictures from his secret office, he was screwed.

Diesel might get a one-way trip back to Alpha-Prime, if he got lucky. If his luck had run out, he could also get a one-way trip to Galactic Gulag XkR-9, one of the worst gulags in the Andromeda Galaxy.

Diesel grabbed the copy of her article, planning to use it for reference as he raced home to do damage control and prepare for whatever Finder's fact-checker showed up to verify or debunk Juliana's claims.

Beneath the surface of his worry about possible discovery, he was quite heartbroken over what he considered Juliana's unexpected betrayal.

Why hadn't she called him? Why hadn't she told

him about her memories of the Defender? How could she remember being shot with Cam's foolproof memory erasing weapon in the first place? Had this alien article been her intent all along? Had the bank robber notes only been a clever ruse to throw him off guard?

He read the part about being shot with an invisible ray gun that made her black out for a short time and upon waking her memories were gone, but over time they'd all come back.

Diesel had never had a chance to look up the circumstances during testing as to the understandable reason it had not worked as expected on one of the test subjects. And he didn't have time to look it up when he pulled into the truck stop parking lot either.

He got out of his truck and realized it was too late to do anything except deflect and react. An older man in jeans and an untucked orange, button-up shirt was getting out of a car, notepad in hand. That in and of itself wouldn't have been alarming except for the bumper sticker by his license plate that read: *If it's not in a Finder's, it's not a Keeper*.

Diesel marched over to the man and asked him directly, "Are you from Finder's?"

The man was older, hair graying at his temples, but still nice-looking. Diesel's despondence over Juliana's betrayal didn't preclude him from being jealous of this man she'd sold her story to.

"How do you know that?" he asked, sounding suspicious.

Diesel pointed to the back of his car. "I saw your bumper sticker."

The man brightened. "Oh! Well, then. Yes, I do work for Finder's. My name is Pete Harriman. Call me Pete."

"Okay. What are you doing here, Pete?" Diesel asked, "Are you in search of a big story about aliens?" He laughed as if it was a huge joke to look for aliens in a place called Alienn.

The man pretended to be amused, but Diesel could tell he was caught by surprise by Diesel bringing up the aliens angle first. Good. That was his intention.

"Sort of, but not exactly. Do you know anything about the rumors here in town?"

"Rumors? What rumors are you talking about?"

"I heard about an *incident,* I guess you'd call it, involving a dangerous creature roaming the streets of Alienn, causing all sorts of mayhem."

"Oh, you mean our local Bigfoot story, the supposedly *true* legend of the Fouke Monster?" Diesel laughed again. "That was just a story way back before my time. They say it's true, but that was a long time ago. I think there is a movie about it, though. You might want to check that out."

"No. Not that one," Pete said. "I heard that there was a malevolent beast roaming around town that had to be subdued with what I understand ended up being experimental tactical means."

"Experimental tactical means? Like a test solution? I've never heard anything like that." *From any human anyway.* As far as Diesel knew, Harriman had not heard it from Juliana, either. She hadn't put anything like that in her article.

The article he'd read from first page to last, standing alone in her empty apartment as his heart sank to his knees. She'd only mentioned the part about a beast roaming around, what they'd called the Boogieman Affair, not the special means they'd used to subdue the creature. How did Pete know about it?

"Well, yes. Say, do you work here?"

Diesel nodded. "I'm the manager of this truck stop."

"Wonderful," the man said. "Could I interview you? I'd like to do some follow-up questions on an article someone turned in to me today."

"Sure," Diesel said. "Come on inside to my office and we'll chat." He pulled his communicator off his belt and texted Cam:

> *Bring your Defender and come to my office.*
> *I've got someone you need to zap, pronto.*

Cam responded in seconds.

> *Who are you and what have you done with my brother?*

Diesel rolled his eyes, stopping in mid-roll. *Space*

potatoes! He didn't need to start that bad habit again. He closed his eyes briefly, opened them and responded with:

> *Just get to my office! Be the solution not the problem.*

Diesel led Pete into the convenience store, walking right past Alice at the front counter. She waved, looking a bit nervous, and started to say something. He held up his hand, pointed a thumb over his shoulder at Pete, and said, "Later, okay? I have a meeting."

Alice nodded, but didn't look happy.

Welcome to my world, he thought bitterly. Diesel didn't expect he'd ever be happy again.

Cam was waiting at his office door with a large Defender hooked on his belt.

Diesel said, "This is our security manager, Cam."

Before he could finish the introduction, Pete stuck his hand out. "Pete Harriman. Call me Pete. Great to meet you, Cam. Interesting place you all have here."

"Thanks, Pete," Cam said. He casually put his hand on his Defender out of Pete's view. Diesel opened the office door, ushering both men inside and gesturing for Pete to sit on the chair across from his desk. It would be easier when Cam fired the Defender and Pete passed out. They wouldn't have to pull his dead weight off the office floor.

Diesel sat behind his desk and Cam positioned himself at the door, just behind Pete and out of his view. Pete seated himself across from Diesel and said, "I sent someone here a while back to possibly get the scoop on a rumor I'd heard about a creature roaming the streets of Alienn."

"Oh? Where did you hear that story?" Diesel leaned forward, elbows on his desk, hands folded together, trying to look casual.

Pete crossed one ankle over his knee and craned his neck sideways to look at Cam before turning back to Diesel. "Actually, I was in a bar in Doraydo about a month ago. This old guy came stumbling in. He was already pretty well oiled, if you know what I mean."

"You mean he was already drunk?" Cam asked, always wanting complete clarity.

Pete nodded. "Yep. So this old guy plops himself down at the only seat available at the bar. It just happened to be next to me. Anyway, he orders his first drink and once he downed it and asked for a second, he suddenly said he knew a bunch of secrets about the town of Alienn and did I want to pay him *scads of cash* for the lowdown for an insider's view of the goings on there."

Diesel and Cam shared a look. "And *did* you pay him scads of cash?" Diesel asked. He and his brother both knew a guy in Alienn who always wanted someone to pay him *scads of cash* for something. It was one of Aunt Dixie's friends from the old folks' home. Norman was as unique a person as their aunt, only he was usually inebriated by noon every day.

"Nah. Told him I didn't have any money." Pete shrugged. "But then he started telling his crazy story anyway."

"If you thought it was crazy, why did you listen?" Cam asked.

"Well, he was sitting right next to me at the bar. The place was packed and there wasn't any other place to go."

Cam's face was a mask of fury when he asked, "So this old guy was spouting this story to an entire crowd?"

Pete shook his head. "No one else was listening to him. Or they couldn't hear him. Either way, after the first story, he started yelling that he needed scads of cash so he could pay for more drinks. The bartender hauled him out after his second shot of whiskey because he could only pay for one. Later, I got to thinking. What if the old guy was talking about something that really happened but it was covered up?"

"The old man said it was covered up?" Cam's frown grew more pronounced and his hand twitched on the handle grip of his Defender.

"Not exactly. He said something like, 'When the Defender didn't work, they all talked about using a bomb,' but then the old guy said that the powers in charge decided against it because their *bomb* wasn't guaranteed to work and also harder to cover up and explain. That really got my attention, know what I mean?"

Cam's lips mashed together for a moment. "What did this guy look like? He sounds like maybe he escaped from his caregivers, know what *I* mean?"

Pete looked down at his notebook and shoved it into his inner jacket pocket. "To tell you the truth, I thought the same thing at first. The old guy was probably crazy or off his meds. So that's why I handed it off to someone else to investigate. In case it was all bogus. I didn't want to waste my valuable time, know what I mean?"

"Got it, but who was it that you turned it over to?" Diesel asked as if he didn't care one way or the other.

He shrugged. "Some young thing I felt sorry for. I used to be one of her instructors when she went to college in Doraydo. We ran into each other, got to talking and she said she was looking for some quick cash to take a trip and research her orphan past or some such foolishness. Anyway, I told her if she found any scrap of information or even any innuendo regarding aliens in this town that I'd pay her big bucks for an article in the next Finder's book."

Diesel pushed out a quiet breath. "So that's why you're here in Alienn? Checking up on her work?"

Pete nodded. "Sort of."

"Sort of? What does that mean?" Diesel asked. Cam had soundlessly moved closer behind Pete. He pulled his Defender off his belt and lifted the weapon, aiming at Pete's back.

Pete said, "Well, the story she turned in wasn't about aliens, it was about bank robbers from over eighty years ago. Like *that* would sell anything in a Finder's book." He shook his head like he pitied her.

Diesel kept his composure, even though he was stunned. Juliana hadn't turned in an article about aliens. She hadn't told the secrets she knew. She'd written the article, but hadn't turned it in. He looked at Cam, who seemed calm. A warm spot started growing from Diesel's heart outward to his chest. Juliana hadn't betrayed him or Alienn. She'd done so at her own expense.

Pete said, "So I came here myself to check it out in case she missed something about the alien story I really wanted."

Cam put his Defender back on his belt and quietly resumed his position by the door. The brothers shared an amused look.

Diesel asked, "What was wrong with the bank robber article she turned in?"

Pete shrugged. "There wasn't anything wrong with it, exactly. Don't get me wrong, she's a good enough writer and all, but the subject matter for the next special edition Finder's book is supposed to be unusual findings in unusual places, know what I mean?" His exasperated expression said it all.

"Bank robbers didn't qualify, huh?"

"I guess it will do if there's nothing else, but I really had my heart set on aliens, know what I mean?" Pete flashed a grin. "Don't suppose the two of you could help me out with that creepy alien story? I could pay you the big bucks instead."

Cam shook his head. "Sorry. I heard it was a wounded dog and the whole alien story was made up from the beginning."

Diesel nodded. "Yep. That's what I heard, too. Sorry we can't help you."

Pete, who'd been congenial the entire time since they'd met, got a very sudden, evil glint in his eye. "You two wouldn't be keeping anything from me, now would you?"

Cam huffed, but remained silent.

Diesel said, "What could we be keeping from you?"

Pete reached into his jacket pocket and pulled out a picture, flipping it face-up onto Diesel's desk.

"If aliens don't roam around here in plain sight causing mischief, what is this half octopus half man looking creature doing in your private employee's only parking lot?"

Chapter 18

Juliana drove back to her apartment, disappointed that Mr. Harriman hadn't cared for the article she turned in. He wanted aliens. His heart had been set on proof of extraterrestrials and nothing else, it seemed, would do.

The secret source he'd referenced—but wouldn't put her in contact with—had been the driving force in his zeal to prove aliens did exist.

Instead, Juliana had given him infamous bank robbers from the last century robbing a bank no one in history had ever heard of, really only proving that they'd been seen and photographed drinking in a speakeasy in the same building.

She felt it was compelling enough and worthy of print.

If Mr. Harriman had seen the alien article she'd written on the proof she had, likely he would have been ecstatic and handed over the chunk of money she was promised to use for the research trip she wanted to take.

But when push came to shove, she couldn't do

it. She couldn't betray Diesel and his family, no matter what he'd done to her heart.

Juliana hadn't been able to deliver the article Mr. Harriman wanted that stated aliens had been living in Alienn, Arkansas for decades. She also hadn't brought him the pictures she'd stolen from Diesel's secret office because she knew it would be disloyal to his whole big family. She just couldn't do it. It wasn't her style to hurt others to further herself or her career.

Standing in front of the two articles, Juliana knew that even if Diesel had used her horribly, she couldn't use him in return.

A slim part of her hopeful soul still believed that perhaps it was a misunderstanding. She hadn't spoken to him all week, but she hadn't tried to call him either. In fact, Juliana still loved him even if he was no longer interested in a future with her. How foolish and pathetic was that? Maybe a lot, but she wasn't going to blow things up forever until she spoke to Diesel in person or on the phone to discover his intentions or lack thereof.

She'd made her decision, snagged the bank robber article and ultimately consigned herself to being turned down by Mr. Harriman. She'd have to wait much longer to finance a research trip to the northwest in search of her family. Any story not containing proof of aliens was never going to be accepted. She'd known that the moment she selected the bank robbers article to deliver.

Mr. Harriman told her he was quite disappointed with her non-aliens article. After listening to him go on about why she hadn't discovered what was truly going on, he'd gone off on a tangent regarding her career, telling her that basically it was over as far as Finder's was concerned. At the end of his rant, he'd dismissed her and told her to take her foolish article about bank robbers with her.

Juliana had been rather discouraged after being ripped up one side and down the other by her former instructor.

But one other thing had happened that gave her renewed hope as far as her relationship with Diesel was concerned.

In her effort to perk herself up without caffeine, she'd thought about Diesel and the events of the past week. Every single one of the recollections she'd thought were dreams after being blasted with the Defender those two times had come back as full-fledged memories. Even when she'd been slack in Diesel's arms, she remembered hearing the conversations between Diesel and Cam.

She didn't even resent Cam for being the shooter. He was only trying to protect his family and the enterprise they ran. Diesel had been upset by the means necessary, but had gone along for the greater good. She understood. The phrase *blood is thicker than water* was accurate for a reason.

The letters she'd read on Diesel's secret desk

regarding Adele and her poor treatment became the thing that was suspect. What if someone, like possibly the apple-throwing menace, had set her up? What if she'd been meant to find those possibly *fake* letters to get her to leave Diesel and never look back? Wasn't that what the mild threat was aiming for this whole time? *Leave my love interest alone or else?*

Juliana needed to ensure exactly how Diesel felt about her before she made any decisions about their relationship. She planned another trip to the Big Bang Truck Stop. She would wait until he spoke to her in person to glean his true feelings.

Her heart was in danger of being further trampled, but she had to know firsthand and not through someone's poisoned pen letter scheme or from apples hurled at her door.

Diesel had been protective of her both times the Defender had been used on her. Would he be so concerned if he only planned to use her and dump her?

Miss Penny poked her head out of her apartment as Juliana approached her door. "I heard you race out of here earlier. Did you make it in time to turn in your article?"

"Yes. But he didn't want it."

"Don't worry, dear. It's his loss," Miss Penny stated plainly and then closed her door.

Juliana smiled and shook her head. She turned the knob of her unlocked door, knowing she'd forgotten to lock it in her zeal to make it to the meeting with Mr. Harriman, which had been a complete waste of time, as it turned out.

Maybe she'd try to get her infamous last-century bank robbers story published somewhere else. Maybe there was a historical society somewhere that would relish the possibility of new information in that regard. She perked up as she stepped across the threshold into her apartment but went cold the moment she closed the door. Something seemed off.

Was someone here? Waiting for her? Half-eaten apple in hand ready to throw? *So foolish not to lock the door.*

"Hello," she called out, desperately hoping no one answered.

She dropped her purse and the unwanted article on the table behind the sofa just as she realized what was wrong.

The alien story was not on the table where she'd left it. Where was it? She looked all around and saw nothing. Juliana dropped to her knees to search the floor, beneath the sofa, every inch of the living room. It was not anywhere in the room. She shifted furniture and chairs just to ensure the pages hadn't slipped through some hidden place. Nothing.

A very horrible thought suddenly occurred. What if the apple-throwing, poison pen menace had gotten hold of her article? What if they'd come inside her home and found it? What if they'd taken it to be publicly distributed?

Wait. Surely her nemesis wouldn't distribute it to the public. But if this person took it to Diesel and said, "Look what Juliana did," that would seal her doom with regard to their relationship. Wouldn't it? What could she do?

Then again, what if it *had* been taken by someone else? Dread ran down her spine in a dark rush of fear at the possibility Mr. Harriman had somehow gotten his hands on it or sent someone to retrieve it from her apartment.

Juliana grabbed her purse. All she could do was warn Diesel and hope he'd agree to speak with her, even if it was only to ensure he knew she hadn't intended for the alien article to get out in public.

Diesel looked at the picture and did his level best not to react. Pete wanted horror and shock and denials. Diesel did the exact opposite. He laughed out loud as if totally amused by Pete's lame attempt to try to prove aliens were hiding in plain sight with this foolish picture.

Pete looked dismayed. "What at you laughing at? I don't think seeing a horrible alien creature roaming around hurting people is a laughing matter."

Diesel pointed to the picture. "That's not a

horrible alien creature roaming around hurting people."

"Oh? What is it then?"

Cam walked over to the desk and looked down at the picture. He chuckled as well. Diesel glanced at his typically very serious brother and together they laughed once more.

"What is so hilarious?" Pete demanded.

Cam cleared his throat and said, "That is a fake alien created as an update to our space-themed marketing strategy to possibly take the place of Maxwell the Martian on our billboards."

"I don't believe it."

Diesel shrugged. "Well, you don't have to, but I'm warning you that you'll look very foolish if you don't."

"Show me. I want to see the fake costume."

"Are you from Missouri or something?" Cam asked. "Missouri is the Show Me state, you know, not Arkansas."

"Ha, ha. Very amusing," Pete said, sitting straighter in his chair. "You will either show me this fake costume right this second, or I'll go public with my suspicions. We can let the readers decide the truth of the matter."

Diesel pushed a button on his intercom. "Nova, would you call Jack and Wheeler into my office? Tell them to bring the latest mascot costume with them, okay?"

"Will do," Nova said, adding, "Also, Gage

wants to speak to you about some test results you asked for and Alice has been waiting all day to talk to you about something personal, but very important, according to her."

"Send in the mascot costume first. Everything else has to wait until later."

Nova pushed out a long sigh and replied, "Okie dokie, Smoky."

Diesel closed his eyes. He knew that was Nova shorthand and it meant Gage and Alice had what she considered important news to impart. He noted her concerns mentally, but it was more important to get rid of Pete and his pet project of discovering that aliens truly did exist. It was Aliens Hiding in Plain Sight 101.

A few minutes later there was a knock at the door. Cam opened it and a half octopus-half man entered through the doorway, two of his tentacles waving in the air. "Take me to your leader or I'll bite you really hard!"

Pete stood up and screamed, backing away from the creature. "Stay away from me!" He rushed around the desk to Diesel's side. "Use the weapon! Use the weapon!"

The creature waved his tentacles again and said, "I'm just kidding. I don't bite very hard, if ever." He then pulled the blobby octopus head off, revealing the face of Diesel's youngest brother, Jack. Behind him, Wheeler walked into the room with a satisfied smile on his face. Wheeler, his artistic brother, and Jack, his *I'm-up-for-anything* brother, had completed the project Diesel had assigned them.

The costume looked exactly like the visitor from Moogally who'd instigated Juliana getting zapped by the Defender that first time. Diesel was very impressed with the workmanship Wheeler had put into the costume. It looked real. He'd commissioned it to show to Juliana in case she remembered the incident, but it also worked perfectly in this case.

"Great costume, huh?" Jack said, tucking the octopus head under one tentacle. "We worked for hours and hours on it."

Pete's face went from the color of ash to fire-engine red in seconds. He picked up the picture, glanced at it and then at Jack, his frown deepening.

"Problem?" Cam asked.

"No," Pete said after a long pause. "It looks exactly like the picture."

Diesel stood up from his desk. "Sorry to cut this meeting short, Pete, but I have a full schedule today." He extended his hand.

Pete shook his hand limply, walked a wide path around Jack, and exited the room as if his butt was on fire. Good riddance to bad rubbish.

Diesel said, "Great job you two. Truly above and beyond the call of duty. I'm grateful."

"Thanks. This was a great project," Wheeler said.

Cam turned to Jack with a smirk. "Take me to your leader, Jack? Really?"

Jack laughed. "It was the first thing that came to mind."

"It was funny, Cam. Lighten up," Diesel said as Jack and Wheeler left his office.

Cam shut the door behind them, but there was an immediate knock. Nova opened the door without invitation and entered. Right behind her was Alice with an anxious expression on her face.

"Nova. Come on in." Diesel tried not to sound sarcastic, but didn't think he pulled it off.

"Alice really needs to talk to you. And Gage wants to bring you the results of some test he did for you and he seems rather excited about it."

"Gage doesn't often get excited about stuff," Diesel said.

Nova nodded. "That's why I think you should talk to him next."

Diesel remembered what he'd asked his brother to test and wondered if what Alice was about to tell him would confirm it. "Call him up and send him in when he gets here."

"Will do." Nova left the room. Diesel signaled Cam to stay.

"What can I do for you, Alice?"

She glanced at Cam before turning her attention to him. "I might have some information about something that is going on."

"What info, and regarding *what* going on?" Cam

asked. "There is lots of stuff going on right now. Could you be a bit more specific?"

Alice looked like she was terrified of Cam and clammed up. Her lips flattened like she'd rather run screaming from the room than speak again.

Diesel asked, "Is it in regard to who might be throwing apples at my girlfriend's doorstep?"

Her eyes widened. "Yes. That's right. How did you know?"

Diesel smiled. "I know things."

Cam, seeming rather impatient with the whole process, asked, "Are you the one who has been doing this?"

Alice's face turned tomato red. "No! Not me! My cousin Adele…um…might be the one doing it."

"Adele?" Cam's brows creased. "She works for me in security downstairs."

"Yes." Alice nodded. "And for as long as I can remember, she's had a huge crush on Our Fearless Leader."

"Really?" He pointed a thumb at Diesel. "Him?" Cam looked shocked.

Alice nodded solemnly.

"I'll try not to be insulted by your amazement," Diesel said to Cam.

"What do you think she did?" Cam asked Alice.

"I can't prove it, but I heard her threaten to toss a bushel of apples on Our Fearless Leader's girlfriend's doorstep to scare her off."

Diesel and Cam shared another look.

"I know she followed her home the first night she came here, so Adele would know where she lived."

"Anything else?" Cam asked.

Alice hesitated. "She's broken into your house, Fearless Leader. I'm sorry not to have come forward sooner with the apple thing, but when I heard her bragging that she broke into your house and could get in there any time she wanted, I realized she'd gone too far with this whole crush thing."

"What did she break into my home to do?" Diesel didn't remember noticing anything out of place or missing.

Alice shrugged. "I'm not certain. All I know is that after the first two attempts with the apples didn't work, she moved on to a plan to break the two of you up. I don't know the details just that she planned to plant evidence for your girlfriend to find."

"What evidence did she have to do that?"

"I don't know, but she seemed rather proud of herself. After the UFO crash in Georgia, she said her plan was working. And she came back with flowers that apparently you sent to your girlfriend on Monday."

"What?"

"She saw the delivery guy walking to your girlfriend's door and intercepted him, pretending to be your girlfriend. The guy gave Adele the flowers and the note you sent."

Diesel shook his head. Juliana hadn't gotten the flowers and that was likely why she never called to comment on them.

Alice continued, "I don't know what she planted in your home, but she said that if it didn't work, she was going to use a still picture she'd swiped of your girlfriend seeing that drunk Moogally resident and send it to someone to make her look so bad that you'd have to remove her from your life. And again, I'm truly sorry I didn't come forward sooner."

Diesel tilted his head to one side. "I appreciate you coming forward with this, given that Adele is your cousin, but I'm confused. Adele has never once approached me in any romantic way."

"Really?" Alice looked surprised. "Didn't you go out with her once?"

Diesel shook his head. "Nope. Never did."

"Huh. I got the impression that you had eaten with her at the Cosmos Café once. She used to talk about it all the time."

Diesel cocked his head, trying to remember any contact with Adele, a person he might not even recognize if he fell over her. Cam spoke up. "You sort of had lunch with Adele."

"When?"

"About eight months ago or so. I was eating at the Cosmos Café with a couple of my people and you came in and sat with us."

Diesel scanned his memory. "Oh. Right. Yes. I

do vaguely remember that. You had two new employees with you, but I sat across from you and we discussed security of the lower level, as usual. Then I recall you also wanted permission to work on a Defender bomb."

"Yep. That's the time. Adele was sitting next to you. I guess you made a bigger impression than either of us was aware of."

Diesel remembered a girl with dark hair and that was about it. "I never even spoke to her beyond, 'Hello, nice to meet you,' though."

Alice said, "She was in love with you from that moment."

"She never said anything to me."

"I think she wanted *you* to make the first move," Alice said. "You were always busy, but you also never seemed to be involved with anyone else. There are rumors it was because of an arranged marriage.

"But when the earthling came in asking about aliens in town and everything, Adele was on duty and she saw all the camera footage. She saw you kiss the earthling and she's been a little strange since."

Cam said, "Thanks for telling us, Alice. I'll talk to Adele and see what else she's done in the name of love. She should never have swiped the photo of the Moogally visitor to give to a human for any reason."

"You aren't going to fire her, are you?" Alice asked. "Please don't fire her because of me."

Cam put a hand on her shoulder. "Your name won't come up, I promise. But I can prove that a picture from our surveillance was given to a human outside of this facility and Adele had access to that file. She'll have to face the consequences of her actions, whatever they are."

Alice pushed out a long sigh. "All right. But keep in mind she was just a girl with a crush on a guy."

Diesel saw Cam roll his eyes. Not surprising for *Mr. I'm-never-getting-married.*

"Thank you, Alice." Diesel said. "I appreciate that you stepped up to do what's right."

Alice nodded and left the room.

Cam said, "I'll take care of this. Also, I'm sorry your girlfriend was threatened."

"Thanks, Cam." His brother walked out, too.

He expected Nova to be right in with Gage. When seconds stretched into a minute, Diesel figured she must have had to fetch Gage from downstairs.

Fine with me. Diesel could use a couple of minutes to himself. He reseated himself behind his desk and noticed that Pete had left his picture of the Moogally resident behind.

Little did he know he'd had the real deal. Diesel smiled.

He reached for the picture, but before he touched it there was another quick knock at his door. He expected Gage with a report, ready to explain the detailed DNA analysis Diesel had requested on one of the apples thrown at Juliana's doorstep. The report was moot now. Adele had been responsible.

Diesel didn't even have a chance to tell the knocker to enter when someone slipped inside, and it wasn't Gage.

"Juliana?"

Chapter 19

Juliana raced toward Alienn, hoping she wouldn't get pulled over for speeding, and terrified that Diesel wouldn't even see her so she could warn him. Perhaps she needed to sneak inside his office and wait it out. Would he even be in there? Could she get past his sharp-eyed receptionist? She'd be the biggest challenge.

As Juliana pulled into the parking lot of The Big Bang Truck Stop, she saw Mr. Harriman race out of the convenience store and leap into his car. He sped away as if his life depended on how fast he departed the area.

He was likely here trying to prove aliens existed in a last-ditch effort to put what he wanted in the Finder's book. He was probably racing away to file the alien story and ruin everything.

Juliana needed to go in and wait for Diesel in his office so she could explain Mr. Harriman had likely stolen the article from her and she was sorry. She just had to sneak inside.

She parked at the side of the building, turned

the ignition off and worked through a quick plan. Juliana rifled through her purse and found some large sunglasses, slipping them on. In her trunk, she grabbed a straw hat she'd used once during a day in the sun picking strawberries. She also had a flowered scarf in the back seat that she wrapped around her neck in her best effort to be incognito.

Juliana strolled slowly to the doors of the convenience store and walked in. The clerk was a young man she'd never seen before. He greeted her politely. She didn't speak, just lifted her hand, waved her fingers in a regal way and moved toward the back of the store in a leisurely fashion, picking up a few things from the shelves and putting them back as if uncertain what she intended to buy.

She made her way to the hallway where Maxwell the Martian resided in his box, sliding quickly down the hall when she didn't see or hear anyone around. Her big plan was to slip quietly into Diesel's office and wait for him to arrive. She could tell him about her stolen article, but more than that, she wanted to assess his feelings for her. Was he finished with her just like he had been with Adele after a couple of days, like in the letter she'd written? Or had those letters been phony? Juliana wished with all her heart for the latter.

She peeked around the corner. Miraculously, Nova's desk was empty, but she heard voices approaching from somewhere. Juliana darted toward the hallway leading to Diesel's office and knocked quickly, not waiting for or expecting an answer.

Juliana didn't even have her hand off the doorknob when Diesel said, "Juliana?" She jumped at the sound of his surprised voice, spinning in place to see him seated at his desk.

"Diesel." She almost asked him what he was doing in here. Duh. It was his office.

He stood and came around the desk. She backed up into the door, unsure of what to expect. Would he be angry? Would he throw her out?

In two strides he loomed over her, not smiling exactly, but not frowning either. He leaned close and whispered, "Why did you turn in the bank robber story when Pete so desperately wanted an exposé on aliens to put in his Finder's special edition?"

Juliana swallowed hard. "Even if you don't want me anymore, I didn't want your family to be hurt. And…well…I guess I didn't want you to suffer either."

"You think I don't want you anymore?" he asked, sounding truly puzzled. "Why?"

"I read the letters Adele sent to you."

"What letters?" His brows furrowed. She'd never seen him look so fierce.

She swallowed hard again. "Well…the ones on your secret desk, in the secret place in your home office right behind the Maxwell the Martian picture."

He leaned closer, but they still weren't touching. He smelled great. She was still worried that the letters were accurate. He hadn't kissed her yet.

"How did you find my hidey-hole anyway?"

"Your Maxwell picture wasn't straight. So I leveled it and, voilà, the door released like I'd said abracadabra or open sesame or whatever magic alien phrase you use. Because you *are* an alien. Right?"

He pushed out a deep breath. "I am."

"From a place called Alpha-Prime?"

"Yes."

"I have to know something else."

"What?"

Tears welled up in her eyes as she asked, "Do you want me anymore? Or is telling a girl you plan to fall madly in love with her just part of your smooth alien moves to lure women into bed?"

"You didn't get my phone message this morning, did you?"

"No." But she'd woken up to the sound of a phone ringing. He must have been the one who called this morning, but when she'd gotten home and saw the article missing, she ran out and hadn't stopped to check her messages.

"I just found out less than ten minutes ago that the note on the flowers I sent you Monday also never made it."

"Flowers? A note?" She shook her head. "I didn't get them."

Her gaze lifted to his eyes and she saw only love and desire in them. He leaned in close and kissed her like his alien life depended on it. His arms wrapped around her and he lifted her off her feet, kissing her deeply and thoroughly.

He broke the kiss only long enough to say, "I have fallen madly in love with you, Juliana." His luscious mouth pressed to her lips, kissing her until she thought she might faint without any help from a Defender.

Her back was pressed to his office door, so when someone started pounding, it felt like it went all the way through her body.

"Who is it?" Diesel demanded.

The only response was further pounding. It made Juliana think about the day Axel had taken her to Diesel's house. Someone had been pounding on his door that day, too.

"Do you think it's the apple menace?" she whispered.

"No. That has been resolved." Diesel lowered her feet to the ground, stepped in front of her to snatch the door open wide enough to peek out.

"What are you—" Diesel's question was cut off when a Defender came through the opening. Juliana saw a female hand around it and a finger on the trigger, which was pulled just as Diesel grabbed it.

There was no noise. No pop. And no gunshot sound. Just silence. Diesel had tried to save her, but

Juliana knew how the Defender worked now and how it impacted her in particular.

She waited for the weapon to render her unconscious. She'd hit the ground, and then not remember anything that just happened for several days. Not their exuberant kisses moments ago. Not that he'd told her he was already madly in love with her. Nothing.

Hopefully, the memories would show up in her dreams eventually and after that they'd become memories. Or perhaps she'd hit her limit of remembering things.

What if being Defender-blasted so many times finally made her lose her memories forever?

Diesel snatched the Defender out of Adele's hand, but not before she managed to pull the trigger. He turned to catch Juliana but something unusual happened. She was still standing. She looked at him quizzically as if she was also shocked to find herself still on her feet.

"Juliana? Are you okay?"

"I think so. Did she not pull the trigger?"

"I thought she did. Perhaps it wasn't charged or something."

"Can that happen?"

He shrugged as a ruckus started out in the hallway beyond his door.

Cam said, "Drop your Defender, Adele."

"No! He's better off with me. We're at least the same species. She's an earthling and inferior!"

Diesel peeked out just as Cam grabbed the young woman by the wrist. "Let go of me," Adele squealed. Cam put a shackle sticker on her wrist and she immediately stopped thrashing around and became compliant. It was the same thing used to subdue the alien in the Boogieman Affair a while back.

Cam said, "Come along, Adele. Be quiet for now. We're going downstairs to talk about all of this."

She didn't say anything, but allowed Cam to lead her downstairs.

Nova popped into the hallway as soon as they were gone.

"Gage is still waiting to see you."

Diesel looked at Juliana. The choice between kissing Juliana senseless and having a conversation with his brother regarding scientific analysis wasn't even a difficult one to make.

"Tell him—"

Gage appeared behind Nova with an expression that was ninety percent excitement and ten percent best day ever.

"I need to talk to you, Diesel. You'll never believe what the results turned up."

"The person who took the bite out of the apple was Adele, right?"

He expected Gage to deflate.

His brother's eyes narrowed for a second. "Yes, but that's not the exciting news."

Diesel pushed out a sigh. "Come on in then." Kissing Juliana would have to wait for scientific analysis courtesy of Gage, his semi-nerdy brother, who lived to explain things.

"Juliana, this is my brother, Gage." She smiled at him. Diesel still hadn't figured out why she hadn't fainted when Adele had fired the Defender.

"Gage, this is my girlfriend, Juliana."

"Really pleased to meet you, Juliana," Gage said with a grin. "I have some news you should also hear."

They all sat down, Diesel and Juliana on his sofa and Gage in a chair.

"The analysis showed not one but two samples on the apple you gave me to test. One was Adele's DNA, as you suspected."

Diesel didn't mean to be impatient, but he was. "And the other turned out to be mine?"

"No."

"It was mine, right?" Juliana said.

Gage nodded. "It was yours, Juliana. Once I figured that out I ran the test five more times to be certain."

"Five more times," Diesel said. "Why on earth would you do that?"

"Because she's part Alpha."

"No way." Diesel was shocked.

"Way." Gage showed him a piece of paper that meant nothing.

"How is that even possible? Tell me."

"I can't prove it yet, but my theory is she's a descendent of the Lost Colony from up in the Northwest."

"What makes you think that?"

"She's got Alpha-Prime royalty in her system."

"Royalty." Diesel looked at Juliana, not smiling exactly, but almost in awe.

"Yep. Isn't that awesome?"

"Sure, awesome." Diesel snapped his fingers. "It that why you think the Defender hasn't worked on her very well?"

Gage nodded. "Probably and once her body gets used to it, likely it will stop working on her altogether. She'll adapt."

Diesel nodded. "She already has."

"I'm part alien," Juliana said and laughed.

"Where are your parents?" Gage asked. "Maybe they just didn't tell you yet."

She sobered immediately. "I don't have any. I'm an orphan."

"Not anymore." Diesel pulled her close and kissed her. He kept kissing her until Gage excused himself and left the room.

Minutes later, Cam barged into his office. "Did you hear what Gage discovered?"

"Go away," Diesel said.

"If what he says is true, she's part of the Lost

Colony and the rumors were true. There *were* survivors from that ill-fated group that landed here so long ago."

"I repeat, Cam. Go away!"

"Aunt Dixie will be euphoric. She's always loved that legend."

Diesel rolled his eyes. "Heaven help us. I can only imagine what schemes she'll come up with to promote Legends of the Lost Colony here in Alienn."

Diesel turned to Juliana. "You know, if what Gage says is true, it's likely you're still considered royalty on Alpha-Prime."

"So?"

"Are you going to want to visit Alpha-Prime, find your kin and possibly marry someone more important than a lowly truck stop manager on a backwater colony planet?" Diesel asked.

"Well, if my choice is limited to some fabulously wealthy, very handsome prince or you, I'll have to think about it, won't I?" She grinned. "Or is that your backhanded way of proposing to me?"

"I want to marry you. I know this is fast, but I've never been more certain of anything in my life." He stared deeply into her eyes. "I think we're meant to be together."

"Can we elope?"

"Elope?"

"Yes. You know, get married quickly?"

"Why are you in a hurry?"

"Well, if we elope then I don't have to worry about some archaic arranged marriage on Alpha-Prime, because I agree with you. We are meant to be together. When we are apart, I don't feel like a whole person, like I'm cold and forgetting something every time I move. Is that strange?"

"No. That's the way I feel, too."

"Is there a justice of the peace in Alienn?"

"Yes."

"Good. Let's go."

"Now?"

"What are we waiting for?"

"Good point."

They were married before anyone could stop them so that they could live happily ever after in Alienn, Arkansas.

Epilogue

Juliana filled the last moving box in her apartment. She'd spent the day getting everything ready to move herself and her life to Diesel's house in Alienn. He was going to pick her up and load these last boxes into his truck for transport to Alienn.

While they'd secretly eloped exactly a week ago, they were also planning a small wedding in another two months to include his entire family. They were waiting for Diesel's parents to return from their travelling and for his sister to get back from an educational training program.

She and Diesel were happy, deliriously so, from her perspective. Not only was a nice wedding in the works so all of his family could attend, they planned to travel to Alpha-Prime in six months. Juliana could discover if she had any distant relatives left there. Royal or not, she didn't care, it was just nice to know she belonged somewhere.

Gage had calculated she was about one eighth Alpha-Prime. Her great-grandmother had been a full alien—like all of the Lost Colony folks before they crash-landed over a hundred and fifty years ago and were never heard from again.

When the Alphas came to Earth to mine for Bauxite and founded Alienn, Arkansas almost fifty years after the Lost Colony disappeared, they sent a team north to investigate, but found no one.

They did find the spacecraft, still hidden beneath a camouflage tarp, and an abandoned camp, suggesting that some of their people survived, but no clue as to where they'd gone. It was assumed they'd perished. The only thing left was the legend.

Her only current worry was Miss Penny. She hadn't heard from her friend all week. Not since she'd told Juliana that Mr. Harriman's refusal of her bank robbery article was his loss.

Once the last box was packed up, Juliana went to knock on Miss Penny's door one last time. She was surprised when it was opened by her landlord.

"What are you doing here?" she asked.

"Miss Penny gave notice."

"Where did she go?"

He shrugged. "I heard she was going into a nursing home. I mean, she looked like she was a hundred years old, don't ya think? Listen, I don't have time to talk. Now I've got two places to get ready to rent." He closed the door on her.

Juliana frowned and stepped back, thinking about where Miss Penny would go. She noticed Diesel pulling into the parking lot with his big truck.

The moment he saw her face he asked, "What's wrong, bride of mine?"

She grinned. "If you keep saying that everyone will know we already got married."

"Everyone already knows except my parents and my sister. I forgot to mention the justice of the peace is one of the biggest gossips in the county. So what's wrong, Juliana? You look worried."

"Miss Penny moved out. I don't know where she went."

He brightened. "What if I know where she is?"

"Do you?"

"My aunt Dixie apparently convinced her to move into the Starlight Old Folks' Home in Alienn. She waved at me. Told me to tell you where she was."

"Interesting. I had no idea she planned to move."

"Well, my aunt already told her we eloped."

"Of course she did. Your aunt is funny."

"Hilarious. Miss Penny said it wouldn't be any fun here without you, so she moved. I think it's a great idea. I figure you would have been worried about her if she stayed here."

"I just wished she'd told me."

"Yeah. Good luck with that. If she's anything

like my aunt, you'll be lucky if you get even one second of warning before the next crazy scheme ensues."

"Good to know."

Later that day, Juliana and Diesel found Miss Penny at her new digs in the Starlight Old Folks' Home. They drove up a long stately drive to the front door. The big brick place, looking like somewhat of a Tudor mansion was on a large lot with a nicely tended green landscape.

"Nice place," Juliana said. "Do the rich and famous of Arkansas live here?"

Diesel laughed. "Not that I know of. The place was donated as a residence for the elderly a long time ago with enough of an endowment for upkeep."

"There you are, Juliana." She looked at Diesel. "Hello, young man. What do you two think of my new home?"

Diesel raised his eyebrows as if suitably impressed and nodded, but didn't say anything.

Juliana said, "I love it, but I was worried about you, Miss Penny. I didn't know you were moving here."

"Miss Dixie Lou Grey told me you'd eloped with this handsome young man you've been seeing." She cackled with glee. "I approve, by the way. Not that you need my permission."

"Well, I'm glad anyway. I hope you'll be happy here."

"Oh, I will. This is a very nice town. I already feel like I belong here. I figured it would be better for me to come here. That way I can still keep an eye on you. In fact, I'll keep an eye on you both."

Diesel said, "My aunt also told me an interesting story about you, Miss Penny."

"Did she now?"

"Turns out you tested as part Alpha-Prime, too, but unlike Juliana, I suspect you already knew it."

Juliana stared between her husband and her friend. "What?"

"It's a long story, child, but suffice it to say, I've been watching out for you since you were born."

Diesel asked, "Were you on the Lost Colony flight that crashed?"

"Well, if I was, I'd be over a hundred and fifty years old by now."

"That doesn't really answer the question Miss Penny. In fact you just answered my question with a question. Have you been taking lessons from my aunt Dixie on how to be wily?"

Miss Penny cackled with glee. "Maybe. I sure do like your aunt. She's a hoot."

Diesel cleared his throat. "So about the Lost Colony flight, will you share your experience?"

"Do you know how old I am, young man?"

Juliana thought it seemed an odd response to Diesel's question.

"I wouldn't even hazard a guess, Miss Penny. My mama taught me it was impolite."

She nodded. "I was a youngster when that craft hit the Earth. I was the daughter of a lady in waiting to the royal princess. A princess who was about to have a baby. I don't know the details because I was too young, but when it was learned the ship was in danger, my mother and I along with the princess and a guard were put in a small life boat and jettisoned.

"The princess went into labor and delivered the baby the moment we landed safely, but she didn't survive."

"Who was the baby?" Juliana asked.

"Your great-grandmother."

"What happened to the guard?" Diesel asked.

"The guard left us before the baby was born to find the other craft and never came back. My mother took me and your great-granny from the site and did the best she could in a world she knew little about, but she had survival skills and she taught me some things, too."

Diesel said, "You are also not all Alpha, are you?"

"No. My mother was all that was left of the shifter race on Alpha-Prime. My father was an Alpha though, except that he died before I was born. My mother and I were the only ones left of our shifter race. It was one of the reasons my mama left to start a new life on Earth. We thought everyone died in the crash and Alpha-Prime decided not to send anyone after us.

"I was raised with your great-granny. I also helped raise your granny and your mama. But when your mama and daddy were killed in an accident there was no one else around and I was too old to take care of you, so I took you to that church. I left a note that said what your name was. And then I kept watch over you. That was what shifters did long ago on Alpha-Prime. We protected the royals we were assigned to."

"Did you fund my scholarships to Missouri and Arkansas?"

"No, no. You earned that all on your own, child. And I was so proud of you. All I did was move to the Midwest and keep on watching."

"Did you ever shift into someone else and talk to me before moving to Arkansas?"

Miss Penny smiled. "No. I didn't want to influence you."

"What changed? Why show yourself when I came here?"

"What changed was me. I'm getting on in years, even for a half Alpha-Shifter. I expect I have another decade or so, but after all these years, I figured it wouldn't hurt to introduce myself."

Juliana was stunned. "You knew my parents, right?"

Miss Penny nodded.

"Then you can tell me all about them."

"That is my plan, dear child. And now that this young man is in your life, I'll expect him to take a blood oath so he can take over for me and keep you safe from now on. My mama performed so I could take over for her. I can do it for your new handsome hubby."

"Blood oath?" Juliana and Diesel asked at the same time, exchanging a dubious glance with each other.

"Either that or we could discuss free milk and cows."

"Blood oath," they both said.

The End.

AVAILABLE NOW

BIKER

BAD BOYS IN BIG TROUBLE 1

Despite the danger, there are some definite pluses to undercover agent Zak Langston's current alias as a mechanic slash low-life criminal. He doesn't have to shave regularly or keep his hair military short. He gets to ride a damn fine Harley. And then there's the sweet, sexy lady next door who likes to sneak peeks at his butt. Yeah, that was a major plus.

Kaitlin Price has had the worst luck with men. As if her unearned reputation as a frigid tease isn't enough, she also has to deal with her stepsister's casual cruelty and taunting tales of sexual conquests she can only dream of. So Kaitlin has never been with a man. So what? So what…

So maybe the sexy bad boy next door would be willing to help her with that.

Gunfire, gangsters and a kidnapping weren't part of her Deflower Kaitlin plan. Good thing for her bad boy Zak is very, very good. At everything.

AVAILABLE NOW

BOUNCER
BAD BOYS IN BIG TROUBLE 2

DEA Agent Reece Langston has spent a year at the city's hottest club, working his way closer to the core of a money laundering operation. Women throw themselves at him all the time, but there's only one he's interested in catching. And she won't even tell him her name.

FBI Agent Jessica Hayes doesn't know much about the sexy stranger except that he's tall, dark and gorgeous. Best of all, he seems just as drawn to her as she is to him—in other words, he's the perfect man to show one kick-ass virgin what sex is all about. No names, no strings and no regrets.

Their one-night stand turns into two. Then a date. Then…maybe more.

Everything is going deliciously well until Jessica's boss orders her to use her lover to further an FBI operation.

Everything is going deliciously well until Reece's handler orders him to use his lover to get closer to his target.

Is their desire enough to match the danger and deception?

BODYGUARD

BAD BOYS IN BIG TROUBLE 3

The baseball stadium is torture for Chloe Wakefield, from the noisy stands to the slimy man her colleague set her up with.

Too bad she isn't with the sexy stud seated on her other side. He shares his popcorn. Shields her from the crowd. And, when the kiss cam swings their way, gives her a lip-lock that knocks her socks into the next county.

Goodbye, vile blind date. Hello, gorgeous stranger.

Staying under the radar is pretty much a job requisite for bodyguard Deke Langston, but he can't resist tasting Chloe's sweet lips. Nor her sweet invitation into her bed, where the sensuous little virgin proceeds to blow his mind.

But someone doesn't like how close they are getting. The thought that scares Deke the most is that another woman in his care might be hurt because of his past.

All of Deke's skills are put to the test as he and Chloe race to solve the puzzle of who is plotting against them.

Chloe's in danger and Deke has never had a more precious body to guard.

AVAILABLE NOW

BOMB TECH
BAD BOYS IN BIG TROUBLE 4

Bomb tech and firefighter Alex Langston has a reputation around the station as a bad-boy, love 'em and leave 'em type, but that couldn't be further from the truth. He wants nothing more than a quiet life after a military tour that saw him in some very hot situations overseas. He garners more than his fair share of feminine attention, but hasn't felt so much as a spark of interest for any woman since landing in Ironwood, Arizona...until now.

Schoolteacher Veronica Quentin was warned to keep her guard up around Alex. The last thing she wants is to be a notch on some sexy stud's bedpost. She's been used before, and knows well the heartache that can bring. But that was before she saw him. And before he rescued her from a mysterious kidnapping that saw her chained half-naked in the town square with a bomb strapped to her chest.

But is Veronica the real target? Or has someone set their sights on Alex?

Until they find out, they can't trust anyone but each other. And the sensual flames that ignite whenever they're together.

BOUNTY HUNTER
BAD BOYS IN BIG TROUBLE 5

Dalton Langston has a sixth sense when it comes to tracking his quarry. He has a talent for getting in his prey's mind. Now, the only thing he's interested in hunting is some rest and relaxation in Las Vegas. The last thing he wants is to get dragged into chasing after some runaway rich girl.

Lina Dragovic has eluded everyone her parents have sent after her in their efforts to force her into an arranged marriage. She's served her time as the Dragovic crime family's cloistered daughter. Now all she wants is her freedom. What better place to hide than Sin City, where the bright lights offer the deepest shadows?

But there's no outrunning the dangerously sexy bounty hunter...especially when getting caught by him is so tempting. And so deliciously rewarding.

Falling in love was never part of the plan.

BANDIT
BAD BOYS IN BIG TROUBLE 6

Miles Turner, a handler and operative with The Organization, a private security firm, is used to always being the man with the plan, the guy in control of everything around him. He can't imagine any situation that would get the better of him—until he meets Sophie.

Travelling sales rep Sophie Rayburn has been burned by love before, but she's determined not to spend Christmas Eve alone. When she spots sexy Miles at a run-down bar in a Podunk New Mexico bar, she decides he'd make the perfect gift to herself. Why shouldn't she indulge them both with a little holiday cheer between the sheets?

Sensual sparks fly as soon as they come together, like they were made for each other, in bed and out. A kidnapping, a drug scam and a dangerous mole don't stand a chance.

Sweet, sexy Sophie is enough to make even a good man lose total control. And Miles is not good. He's all bad boy.

CLOSE ENCOUNTERS OF THE ALIEN KIND
NOCTURNE FALLS UNIVERSE

Pilot. Guard. Prisoner.

All three are crashed in the Georgia woods, lost on a world where extraterrestrials are the stuff of science fiction. Blending into the human world is doable, if dangerous. But what if the locals are far from human themselves, with secrets of their own?

Former bounty hunter Stella Grey grew up an orphan on family-centric Alpha-Prime, so she knows the value of belonging. Leaving everything— and everyone—behind to join distant kin a galaxy away in Alienn, Arkansas, is a small price to pay.

Heading up a retrieval operation following a spacecraft crash in rural Georgia is her chance to prove herself to them. Her mission? Locate the ship's occupants. Secure the prisoner. And, above all, keep the earthlings from discovering that aliens live and walk among them.

Draeken Phoenix is the bad boy from one of Alpha-Prime's best families, known for getting in and out of scrapes with wit, charm and sheer bravado. He never expected to become an actual prisoner bound for a galactic gulag. Until now, the worst thing that had ever happened to him was losing the woman he loved. But he has a plan.

He's bet his life on it.

About the Author

Fiona Roarke is a multi-published author who lives a quiet life with the exception of the characters and stories roaming around in her head. She writes about sexy alpha heroes, using them to launch her first series, Bad Boys in Big Trouble. Next up, a new sci-fi contemporary romance series. When she's not curled on the sofa reading a great book or at the movie theater watching the latest action film, Fiona spends her time writing about the next bad boy (or bad boy alien) who needs his story told.

Nothing's sexier than a good man gone bad boy.

Want to know when Fiona's next book will be available? Sign up for her Newsletter:
http://eepurl.com/bONukX

www.FionaRoarke.com
facebook.com/FionaRoarke
twitter.com/fiona_roarke

Made in the USA
Columbia, SC
20 May 2017